Praise for *Ahalya*

'Ahalya, Draupadi, Kunti, Tara, Mandodari – each of the Pancha Kanyas is fascinating. Ahalya's story has been told and retold several times, sometimes with varying accounts across texts. What was her relationship with Gautam and Indra? What was her crime? How was she redeemed? Why is she among the Pancha Kanyas? There have been modern retellings and interpretations too. Koral Dasgupta's wonderful retelling adds to this corpus, with a lyrical and poetic quality. The image that will remain with you is of the Mist ... Enthralling'

Bibek Debroy

'"Go, woman, find your world yourself. The joy you seek deserves to be discovered." Armed with this advice, Ahalya sets off on her life's journey. The magical and thought-provoking adventure that follows will intrigue and mesmerize readers'

Chitra Banerjee Divakaruni

'Koral Dasgupta's evocation of Ahalya, the first of the Pancha Kanyas, the five virtuous women from Indian myth, is an enigmatic tale about purity, chastity, seduction and redemption, told from the perspective of the eternal feminine'

Namita Gokhale

'Amazing premise and approach. This is one unique take on an age-old tale. Brilliant and intriguing'

Anand Neelakantan

'Impressed. I literally never imagined the interior world of a character from mythology in this way, let alone contemplating this way of reflecting on the soul, embodiment, desire and a woman's experience of the Brahma- and Indra-dominated worlds! Really powerful'

Prof Brian A. Hatcher

'In this original and spirited interpretation of the tale of Ahalya, Koral Dasgupta gives voice, character and agency to an enigmatic and fascinating female figure from ancient Hindu lore, while exploring and seeking to resolve the proverbial and vexing tension between asceticism and sensuality'

Prof Philip Lutgendorf

'Engaging and cinematic narrative'

Srijit Mukherjee

'A stream of consciousness; a spiritual telling. It rescued and redeemed the purity ruse. Koral is a visual writer'

Nabila Jamshed

'A stunning read. Fluent and engaging. What a fine writer!'

Fiona Sampson

'Panchakanya and other women, reinterpreted, is a most pertinent call. *Ahalya* is beautifully written and the little details and imagined conversations bring the character alive. I also enjoyed the almost surrealistic movement between mythical time and ours. It's a reminder that we in India live by a philosophy of transitions, an in-between-ness. Ahalya is amongst us'

Prof Malashri Lal

'Powerful ... The novelty of the novel lies in the fact that no other writer has talked about Ahalya vis-à-vis her womanhood'

Outlook

'In a most intriguing retelling, Dasgupta's narrative turns the seduction story on its head, making Ahalya the seducer instead of the seduced'

Scroll.in

'An ecocritical reading of *Ahalya* reveals the exploration of an ancient connection with nature that's sacred, intimate, and as we are in the midst of an environmental emergency, vital to reconcile with today'

Firstpost

'[T]he brilliance of Dasgupta's retelling is not just within the confines of that transformation itself, but rather, the importance of being seen, validated and loved as you are'

Southern Humanities Review

'Koral Dasgupta creates true wonder with her new book *Ahalya*'

Tempest

'A stunning piece of literature'

Dipannita Sharma

Praise for *Kunti*

'Koral Dasgupta writes about Kunti, one of the Pancha Kanyas, with verve, emotion and passion. Her highly readable account of this fascinating character, who played a key role in the Mahabharata, is a must for those wishing to know about our past and the dialectics of gender within it'

Pavan K. Varma

'Koral Dasgupta makes the ancient myths speak in new and unexpected voices; voices that have been lost and sunken in the dominant narrative consciousness, and yet, the voices of characters who made the flesh, blood and the values of the epics possible'

Saikat Majumdar

'Bringing heroines of yore, like Ahalya and Kunti, to contemporary times, Koral Dasgupta writes with a rare verve and energy. Never dull or pedantic, she makes the woman within the legend come alive. A rare talent'

Makarand R. Paranjape

Praise for *Draupadi*

'*Draupadi* lives up to the expectations set by *Ahalya* and *Kunti* ... Koral [Dasgupta] dares to boldly push the narrative in ways you cannot imagine. A must-read'

Kiran Manral

'This is a striking rewriting of Draupadi's story. Koral Dasgupta has given us a Draupadi who is fearless, politically astute and unwilling to be anyone's victim. This Draupadi leans into her power and changes the course of history in Dasgupta's beautifully crafted world'

Prof Tracy Pintchman

'In poetic prose Koral Dasgupta weaves surprising threads into the ever-evolving tapestry of the Mahabharata, enriching it with this empowering, lyrical telling of Draupadi's life'

Prof Hillary P. Rodrigues

'Koral Dasgupta has given us a unique take on a well-known story from the Mahabharata. It is fascinating to hear this tale from a female perspective, to hear [Draupadi's] thoughts and struggles about being offered in marriage to all five brothers, as well as her eventual realization of the purpose behind the marriage. This work clearly shows Draupadi to be an intelligent and rational player in the divine plan. In our attempts to make the academic world more diverse and accessible to all, a reading of Draupadi alongside the Mahabharata would be an excellent way to open new dialogues in the classroom and beyond'

Prof Arnold Smit

'This lyrical and insightful reimagining of Draupadī's narrative is a worthy entry in the long tradition of telling the tales of India's (and the world's) great epics'

Prof Brian Collins

'A lively series of beloved stories from ancient India that speak to modern readers'

Prof Paul B. Courtright

Praise for *Mandodari*

'Imaginative, intense and insightful ... Narrated in Koral's signature style, the exchanges of Mandodari and Sita (and their implications for Ravan and Ram) are absolutely fascinating'

Ashwin Sanghi

'[*Mandodari*] has several strengths, including, but not limited to, Dasgupta's envisioning of the inner world of the women of Lanka, the differences, sympathies and alliances within, as well as the titular character's moral turbulence'

Telegraph

'*Mandodari* with its lyrical prose and philosophical moorings ... conjures up visions of a mesmerizing world. The book shows how so much is made possible by a lone woman's resilience and unswerving commitment to do the right thing'

New Indian Express

Praise for *Tara*

'Embedded within the epic saga of the Ramayan, *Tara*'s nuanced narrative is bathed in grace and empathy. We enter the non-textual world of the vanaras to discover a deep worldview through the voice of an extraordinary protagonist'

Namita Gokhale

'A powerful depiction of Tara's world, encompassing Bali and Sugreev, with distinct ideologies influencing the rules of the Kishkindha kingdom'

Amish

'Exuberant and imaginative, this narrative about kinship, friendship and love explores questions about borders: between the animal and the human, the wild and the tame, the living and the dead, the revelatory and the remembered, heaven and earth, language and silence. With a cast of vividly etched characters and a feel for the mysteries that lie at the heart of intimacy, here is a fascinating tale by an inventive and thoughtful storyteller'

Arundhathi Subramaniam

KUNTI

KORAL DASGUPTA has published an eclectic range of books, from academic non-fiction to relationship dramas. Her books are discussed in the context of gender studies, art, myth and ecocritical literature. Other than India, Koral's books can be found in the libraries of Harvard University, Columbia University, the University of Pennsylvania, University of Chicago, University of Wales, Duke University, University of North Carolina, Texas A&M University, among others. The books in the Sati series have been nominated for various prestigious awards, with *Ahalya* most recently being recommended for the 2023 Sahitya Akademi Prize Honour List.

Koral is the founder of www.tellmeyourstory.biz and conducts writing programmes and critical thinking workshops for educational and corporate floors. She has been recognized on the Innovator25 Asia Pacific 2019 list prepared by the Holmes Report and featured in the Women of Wonder (WOW) series in *Outlook Business* magazine.

Her website is www.koraldasgupta.com.

Also in the Sati series

Ahalya

Draupadi

Mandodari

Tara

KUNTI

KORAL DASGUPTA

THE SATI SERIES II

PAN

First published 2021 by Pan
an imprint of Pan Macmillan Publishing India Private Limited
707 Kailash Building
26 K. G. Marg, New Delhi 110 001
www.panmacmillan.co.in

Pan Macmillan, 6 Briset Street, Farringdon, London EC1M 5NR
Associated companies throughout the world
www.panmacmillan.com

ISBN 978-93-90742-17-2

12

Typeset in Guardi LT Std by R. Ajith Kumar, New Delhi
Printed and bound at Repro India Limited

FSC
www.fsc.org
MIX
Paper | Supporting responsible forestry
FSC® C047271

For my son, Neev Tanish

CONTENTS

SERIES INTRODUCTION

The Pancha Kanyas of Hindu mythology are Ahalya, Kunti, Draupadi, Mandodari and Tara, while the five Satis include Sita, Sati, Savitri, Damayanti and Arundhati. The distinction between these two different titles arose primarily because certain versions of the epics have taken the liberty to celebrate women as per the popular beliefs of their era and, of course, those of the translators. One school of thought defines 'Sati' as symbolizing the women's unconditional devotion to and dependence on their men. It casts the women as loyal followers, strongly supporting the vision of the men around them or helping them overcome social and emotional challenges. These women are depicted as self-sacrificing and selfless, yet invincible when drafting their own position of strength and authority.

Various senior scholars translate the Pancha Kanyas as 'five virgins'. Thus, based on textual evidence, the Kanyas and Satis are different women. However, in the earliest texts, there is no mention of the Pancha Satis; they only talk about the Pancha Kanyas who are deemed as the Maha Satis. Even in regional interpretations, especially in some eastern and southern states of the country, this division is blurred. This could be due to the difference in the spread of the Mahabharat of Vedavyasa versus the dissemination of Valmiki Ramayan. The former specifically mentions the Pancha Kanyas.

Many versions of the Ramayan discuss the Satis in terms of loyalty and physical chastity. Such women, including Sita, aren't restricted to only five. But they don't club them under the umbrella term, Pancha Sati. In my own studies, I came across some scholarly assumptions that the Satis were reborn as Kanyas, with research trying to draw parallels!

An ancient *shloka* establishes that reciting the names of the Pancha Kanya can dispel sins, which again confirms the 'Sati' status of these women. Sati, meaning pure, devoted and fair. Purity that cannot be destroyed by external influence, because criticism or judgment cannot deflect one from her chosen path of righteousness.

In the Sati series, I follow this conception of 'purity' while retelling the stories of the five illustrious women: Ahalya, Kunti, Draupadi, Mandodari and Tara. The purity that is brave enough to present itself the way it is – sans any cosmetic cover – and mirrors the mind unpretentiously as much as it exposes the politics of a society.

However, the Sati series is not meant to be biographical. The purpose of the series is to draw attention to a part of the journeys of these legendary women that have been grossly overlooked. Identities have been imposed based on incidents that the patriarchy considered criminal, shameful or irresponsible. When these known events adopt the narrative voice of a feminine titular character, the stories change. The world expands. The Sati series not only presents an inclusive overview of the protagonist's own life but also dives deep into the suppressed pain of those around them – be it a man or a woman.

In the first, fourth and fifth book of the series, *Ahalya, Mandodari* and *Tara,* the entire narrative had to be recreated. About Kunti and Draupadi, a lot is known already. My retellings spotlight the making of these characters, albeit from a non-traditional perspective, which ushers the readers into a new era of thinking and reimagining.

Ahalya introduced the woman as a lover. Ambitious, futuristic, royal and calculative; not afraid to express, nor hesitant to ignore the binding rules of the world. *Kunti* called for a relook at the patriarchal origins of 'Mata' and, in relation, the pervasive sociopolitical image of the sacrificing Indian mother. *Draupadi* was even more complicated than the previous books because it shed light on the societal reactions across generations towards crimes against women, particularly those who are successful. *Mandodari* sparked yet another powerful discourse on the critical choices faced by an accomplished woman between the calls of of her mind and heart, in light of a terrible sin committed by her extremely talented husband. *Tara,* the last book of the series, brings up the discourse of human–animal politics, highlighting the grandeur of certain traditions of the forest and the wisdom of animals that transcends boundaries. It also explores the sensitivity that prompts a woman to forgo the blinds borne by the diplomatic crown of a queen.

Ram's killing of Bali while hiding behind a bush is a disturbing episode from the Ramayan that I personally could never digest. Tara's narrative opens with an acknowledgement of Bali's death and then travels through the sequence of events – securing some emotional and logical derivatives.

PROLOGUE

With a tremendous uproar, lightning split the overcast night sky into glittery fragments. Torrential downpours raised havoc to drown the long-denied thirst of a withered drought. It felt like the jubilance of nature rather than the ravage of the forces. This wasn't just clouds, pregnant with water, releasing their weight while thunder cracked in the sky. Nature exploding in uproarious celebration led me on to the tree of mirth, its overwhelming branches bent with celestial blooms trembling in the wind. So were my insides. Little sockets smoothened by heavenly footsteps had fireflies flying in and out, lighting the way to the top, where the trunk spread its wondrous, colossal boughs. Surrendering to the pleasure, I tried to investigate the excitement of the ambience. Aggressive winds blew away every particle of tar that may have settled on my skin in the course of life, abrading the grease off the surface. The moisture in the air hydrated my body, after days of negligence in the dense forests. My hair felt wet, the dew dripping from the branches of the Kalpavriksha softening its firm strands. The ill-bred chignon fell back to its bounteous freedom, their unruly length arrested by thick, spiralling threads of jasmine. Showers of sandalwood dust fell on the folds of my attire, lending fragrance and energy. I stepped on the bed of parijata and was immediately veiled inside a transparent bubble. It shook vigorously, but even the strong winds couldn't rupture its thin walls or vandalize the pleasant air inside.

Guards of the sceptical queen fell off after years of restraint. I travelled back to the times when dreams were innocent and the world felt within grasp. Indra looked divine. Had he schemed to entrap my obsessive heart with his aqua skin and lotus fragrance? Or is a lover naturally overpowering? I had started feeling as wonderful as Indra himself, pristine and regal, much unlike the manipulative Kunti – cleansed of all the mud and slime on her body, gathered from the royal corridors and tropical forests.

The deva's foreplay started with many levels of touch. He touched with earnest eyes to uplift my simple presence to the state of undisclosed magnificence. He touched with liberal smiles, before which, all miseries made an unconditional surrender. He touched with a seductive voice, inducing compassion desirous of forgoing all barriers known to keep two individuals apart. The fragrance of his body humbled the clusters of parijata and numbed mortal discomposure into luxurious repose. The teasing petals flew, fell or remained suspended inside the bubble. He hadn't even touched my skin yet!

Alluring steps brought him closer, his eyes narrowed and lowered slightly till my lips, before they moved up to my eyes. The water gushing down the outer wall of the bubble reflected our bodies which were barely a feet away from each other. We made for a breathtaking couple, a union of disproportionate equals! An erudite woman befitting a man of passion. The king of the *devas* and a queen from earth. One, a fierce warrior and the other, an elegant intellectual. The powerful paired with the ambitious!

Indra leaned forward. Briefly, his locks brushed across my shoulder, casting their shadow over my face. Our breathing had picked up pace in response to the intense stimulation. The proximity scorched my forehead every time he exhaled. His hands were left loosely to their whims, free to establish their grip. But he kept flirting with his eyes, drunk on the poison of patience. I closed my eyes, attempting to concentrate on the inner self that had waited for too long to be loved by Indra.

I heard a loud, horrifying crash inside!

In the worthless threats of the winds whirling downwards, I could hear blatant sighs from the past. The sigh of pain, of jealousy, of helplessness. And the sigh of anger. The angst of the feminine. And a mystic curse of the virile. Suddenly losing control, I almost raised my head to stop the source of the obnoxious sensation. Were we being watched? Shocked and suspicious, I looked around restlessly in the sublime expanse lit sparingly by nature.

I could see nothing, no one. Only the interlocking branches of the Kalpavriksha and a swarm of fireflies.

'Deva, do you hear someone? Do you see something?' I asked nervously.

'I see and hear none, but you, Queen!' the melodious voice made me turn, distracted from the concerns that had momentarily seized my attention. Blushing to such alluring indulgence from the celestial, my apprehensions were allayed. With a warm touch on my lower back, Indra gently brought me back to time. His time. My body gave way, the mind went blank again. I fell, only to land in Indra's arms, now locked around my waist. I looked back at him and touched his chest.

He placed me on his knee, looking up at my face with the manner of having met his first love.

Softly and yet with a calm curiosity on the brink of falling apart, he ran the tip of his fingers over the cloth that covered my thigh, on my bare hands and through the long, flowing hair fanned out on my back. At the unconditional attention, all perceptions of beauty deserted me; suddenly, it didn't matter whether I had large eyes or plump lips or a voluptuous body. I was the muse of the lover; I was the need of his heart. I was perfection, whatever that meant.

Or was I?

Eyes of compassion; the touch of desire; the scent of seduction. Who knew better than I that those magical sensations were as nonexistent as Indra himself? That the truth of each moment lost its significance in the next! That this desire wouldn't find possessive lovers to hold on to each other with pledges of inseparability! Haven't I witnessed in the past, the deceit of both human and nature?

*

'Henceforth, my daughter Pritha will be yours. May she be recognized as Kunti, the daughter of Kuntibhoja!'

Father Shurasena's generous offer was received with tearful delight. Too young to understand the shift of custody, I only changed hands. His childless cousin – now my foster father Kuntibhoja – held me like a precious gem, his hands shaking with joy. The Yadavas cheered. Time rushed forward, like it always does.

Sitting on the velvety grass of the huge garden, I was busy remoulding the clay dough into the royal symbols of the Yadavas. My unskilled hands of seven years had still not learnt how to make pointed weapons to scare the brash, disobedient horses. Father helped me carve them, back when I got angry with each failed attempt. On one of those evenings, I suddenly asked, 'Why did King Shurasena give me away?'

Shocked fingers with layers of moist clay on them stopped abruptly. 'Are you unhappy here, Kunti?'

'No,' I shrugged. 'I am just curious.'

Father stared at my little face, exploring the origin of the question. I smiled at him and went back to the dough he had left unfinished. He wouldn't get the answers he was looking for, I was good at hiding them. There is something in the air that only adopted children can feel. You have to be one to know what I mean. Not something you can complain about.

'You are my child, born at his house by mistake. He returned to me what is mine.' Father's voice was resolute. He meant it. I dragged myself closer and sat with our knees touching. He pulled my plaits and we laughed.

'Shouldn't you want your child to be a great conqueror?'

His hands stopped again, this time amused. 'Would you want a conqueror as your child?' He flipped the question back to me.

'I want to be the biggest conqueror. One who can defeat the world and become the mightiest ...'

Kuntibhoja laughed so loud, it almost shook the trees around.

'A conqueror is no more than a brave, ruthless soldier, Kunti.' He said when he calmed down.

'Be an administrator. The administrator decides what is to be conquered, when and how.'

I didn't know what it meant, but I thought about it whenever I could.

From Kuntibhoja, I learnt the discipline of the Brahman and the sophistication of a Kshatriya. 'The Brahman is led by the knowledge of the divine. He doesn't fall to the merits of alien, materialistic impulse,' echoed the deep voice of the royal priest seated in the backyard of the temple. I was set free from his invigilation in the evenings, to spend time with the army general. Once, with my clothes hoisted up to the knees and the loose end girdled around the waist, I overheard him reprimanding a junior soldier.

'The Kshatriya is born to represent a kingdom. We are here to protect the boundaries of lands, not remain besotted by the charm of a newborn flower. Can you now stop lamenting about the buds that fell with the turn of your sword?'

The general turned. I was already in position with my spear.

*

Back in the well-lit abode, a plush bed was ready with a spotless cover, just the way I liked. I placed atop it the readings offered by my teacher. Attendants were around to serve if needed. Friends, I had none. During such isolated hours, I returned to the mesmerizing tale of Ahalya – the remarkable woman whose husband, Maharishi Gautam, had abandoned her upon allegations of adultery with Devraj Indra!

Even after I was done with her story, she would visit the untrodden corridors of my palace – solitary and dreamlike. I would follow the hum of her soft song while walking on the far end of our balconies or plucking fruits from the orchards below. She'd smile at the flies and bathe in the moonlight. When I rushed towards her, she disappeared.

Truth has many versions. It changes from mouth to mouth. It amasses myriad interpretations of the same story to make it sound more convincing to the listener and become her truth. So it was for me. Ahalya's misfortune was supposed to pass doctrines of restraint. I was supposed to fear the power of authority and follow the rituals they called 'virtues'.

'Illusion doesn't have a permanent form; it is destructive to chase it and hence, such pursuits only lead to deeper layers of self-obsession but nothing to live for in reality,' the *Raj Purohit*, the royal priest, explained in vociferous terms. 'Just like Ahalya was fooled by Indra, Gautam left her and she also lost her physical dominance. Ahalya was living her life on a bed of illusions. In the more pragmatic world which counts and measures, she was no more than a reclusive loner!'

Yet, on those early mornings when I looked out of the window, the toddling sun washing the last traces of kohl off the horizon, the mild breeze reshuffling the *shlokas* meticulously arranged in order, my mind would wander across forbidden territories, attempting to inspect another version of all this.

What was Ahalya's truth?

And what made Indra irresistible? That he was handsome? Passionate? Lustful? Skilful?

*

My younger brother, Vasudev, visited often – an energetic, high-spirited child who slowly withdrew into a calm adult as the years passed. The topmost chamber in the palace of my foster father was reserved for me. A dedicated concierge smeared sandalwood on my skin and massaged scented oil into the hair. The Raj Purohit personally attended to my learning of the Vedangas, introducing me to arithmetic, science and language. During the day, I often eavesdropped on my father's conversations and discussions about the estate. Vasudev would mischievously bring my curiosity into the open, alerting the diplomats to their hidden audience. I was unapologetic. Burning inside me was an insatiable quest to investigate the available as well as the forbidden. My father narrowed his eyes but didn't utter a word. In that silence, we signed a treaty – I would maintain strict confidentiality about the acquired information and, in exchange, I would be admitted to the hitherto inaccessible. Soon, his most trusted ministers were assigned to explain the components and computations of *rajneeti* (politics) and *rananeeti* (rules of the war) and *arthaneeti* (economics) to me. I raised questions, sometimes uncomfortable ones. I experimented openly, observing humans through their triumphs and failings. I analysed the results without anyone noticing the disruption.

Knowledge empowers and it also rebels. For the world at large, I was growing up to be a fine young woman in wit and appearance, befitting the elegance of a princess. My presence would intimidate. The privilege of my conversation was available only to a deserving few; it could engage beyond spoken words; my presence would linger even after I had made an exit.

Inside my private chambers, where opulence was boundless and expression was free, I ruminated on the calibre of all such possibilities that weren't socially and politically popular and hence, were left unspoken. After all, why would a woman live in denial of her reality? I reasoned. What was it that Ahalya received from Indra – an invisible lover – that her soul so boldly discarded Gautam, her husband? Why was she not afraid of *adharma*! And as the folklore elaborates, if it was Indra who had committed the deception, how could a woman not differentiate between reality and illusion? Who on earth was not aware of *Indrajala* – a more lethal weapon of the Devraj than his menacing *vajra*!

Question after question piled up. I wanted to know more about Ahalya and her union with the powerful Indra. I researched, I wondered. I asked for the story to be told again and again. The Raj Guru was thrilled that his student was not only a scholar of great brilliance, but also the consumer of preferred morals. If only he knew that the repeated reinforcement erected a castle of desire within her to experience Indra more intensely than Ahalya! Not only as the fantasies of a woman waking up to her adolescence, but also as a scholar driven to pin her academic insights, attempting to enter an undefined illusion. Existing texts revealed the Brahmanical truth of the story. Of giving and sacrificing and conforming – the virtues and vices, painted in black and white. No one asked Ahalya, no one checked with Indra. Everyone believed what was presented by the learned. What was the Kshatriya version – of protecting, aiming and acquiring, more empirically than philosophically?

Once again, who is Indra? A king? A lover? A philanderer?

In Ahalya's songs, I heard the birth of a woman who deserved to be loved. She had been born in Brahma's heart, much before the manifestation of her physical form. Not too different from my story perhaps, as my childless foster father had dreamt up for me, though I wasn't his biological child. The story of Ahalya's marriage made me cringe. I was told she had fulfilled her responsibilities, like any other dutiful wife. I was left astounded by her resilience. Finally, when the king of the devas played out his magic, I couldn't help thinking of it as the best reward bestowed by the divine. Her beauty had received its due. She had managed to absorb every bit of that nectar called love before being silenced into a rock! Why was she silenced? Had her life-force been so daunting for the rest?

*

That evening when Indra and I were together, my moment of truth clashed miserably with Ahalya's. I heard her sigh of pain, of anguish, of jealousy. I breathed out in despair. Wasn't I meant to be her true successor? Before I could address that, I heard resounding laments from the east. Heat waves hit the bubble that had sheltered us in its room. The transparence convulsed but didn't melt. Surya, my friend, my companion, was lighting up dark times. What was the cryptic message he was trying to send me? Wasn't he happy for me?

1

North of Avanti, my foster father's kingdom, was the abode of great wisdom. Learned scholars and accomplished sages would often turn up to immerse themselves in the insightful philosophy that had been passed through generations and multiplied with exchange. Month-long conferences were held at the royal auditorium. Subjects such as trade and business, leadership and aristocracy, philosophy and mathematics, astronomy and astrology were debated by outstanding scholars who enlightened the house with their mutual interchange of knowledge. I distinctly recall the uninvited, unexpected entry of Rishi Durvasa between one such conference.

Who on earth hadn't heard of Durvasa? The hermit notorious for his impatience and illtemper, who had cursed many to an infinite period of misfortune.

Baffled and confused, Father looked at me. I looked back with a reassuring smile; I would take charge and he needn't bother. Not that I wasn't worried. But a Kshatriya doesn't hold back; I didn't either. I bowed before the sage and placed my broad forehead, which as many had opined, showed signs of generous prosperity, on his feet laden with ashes from many lands. He pronounced a blessing to extend my life by a few more years! I held up a silver waterpot, looking at him in the eye. Sharp gestures of the assessor promised there would be rigorous evaluations in the days to come, though he was impressed with the initial welcome. The sheen of the elite had cast its impression but the recluse desired what money couldn't buy.

I showed him upstairs, moving towards the

guest chambers endowed with well-resourced arrangements. He stopped abruptly when a srikarna bird sang to his right and expressed his preference for a far more austere and unfurnished room facing in the northeasterly direction. The room he had asked to be set up in usually remained empty – we called it the *Ishan griha*. The nervous attendants were about to start running to assemble the maharishi's bed inside the sparse room, when they stopped, bewildered, and looked at me for instructions. I dismissed them. Durvasa spread a thin cloth on the ground in front of a huge window facing the morning sun.

'The sage hasn't entered the palace to seek the hospitality of our mahogany bed stands and expensive threads to sleep on.' I sent a note to my father. 'His expectations are either none, which is unlikely, or profound, which need to be decoded with patience.'

Durvasa was liberal with his unexpected demands, keeping me on my toes. I ran helter-skelter putting things together. One moment I was preparing for his morning puja, the next I was all over the palace ponds, gathering lotus. When he meditated with the camphor and coconut husk burning before him, it was my duty to see that the smoke didn't choke him or extinguish. I would go to far lengths to keep the birds, bees and insects away from the vicinity when he desired seclusion. Father would be informed well in advance when I felt that the sage hoped to be attended by the king. After all the chores, when he rested at night, I massaged his feet with warm oil, until he drifted to sleep.

When the attendant brought me a sealed scroll from Vasudev, I rushed through it and left it on my pillow to read again at leisure. He had ridiculed my bustling schedule at present. 'A befitting response awaits, Brother.' I murmured under my breath before running out. The last few words in his note had still stayed with me.

'Born from Shiva's wrath, Durvasa's sudden anger is infamous for bringing untold miseries upon his victims. But isn't Shiva the least demanding God, happy with simplicity in devotion? How would Durvasa be any different?

You have a discovery in waiting, Sister.' The boy was growing up.

Early in the mornings, when Durvasa meditated, I poured water warmed with lotus oil on the hair matted on top of his head. Simple refreshments of milk and fruits were arranged for him between the rituals. With great caution, I tried to peel off that upper, encrusted layer of his skin, which made him violent and scary. What stood before me was a small, whining child, hoping to be attended on priority, imposing upon his company an incredible demand for motherly commitment.

At one such junction, after an unusually hectic monsoon day spent to meet the demands of this childish man, my body wet, soul tired and feet bruised from venturing across uneven terrains, for the first time, Durvasa looked at me with kindness. I knew I had caught a fever. I needed the generous and gentle spread of my bed, tucked away from the harsh commands of the sage. 'Princess, please retire. If he calls, we are there to attend.' My attendants revolted. 'He can't be sending you on more expeditions to fulfil his sadist whims.'

That was when the Ishan griha echoed. 'Kunti ...'

The girls around me were shocked into silence, in panic over which one of them would have to enter the room in my absence. Skin burning with temperature, body shivering to an abnormal cold, I shoved them aside.

That evening, Rishi Durvasa looked up with unforeseen fondness and invited me to sit near him. From his little cloth bag, he pulled out some seeds and weeds, and asked for some spices from the royal kitchen. Half unconscious, I bleakly opened my eyes once. He was grinding something in haste. In the earthen lamp placed near him, he had dropped some turmeric and cinnamon in the oil and god knows what else. The aroma felt warm and soothing to my flowing nose. He prepared a solution and poured it inside my mouth. The taste buds revolted, my eyes came together with great discontent at the bitterness and acridity of the medicinal concoction. The liquid rendered me motionless, almost cutting me off from all kinds of stress, my consciousness drifting into temporary non-existence. For days, I had been deprived of a calming repose. This evening, my body had given up, though my spirit had not.

I woke up in the late hours of the night to a faint music. It seemed like a divine therapy providing strength to the ribs. A melodious mantra with energetic words presented with thrust seemed to permeate through my skin, without meddling with the tranquillity of the night. The head felt lighter, the throat went back to its vigour, the feet hoping to take a grip of the ground, I looked around and sat up like I had been struck by lightning. The melodious mantra and healed body were not the hallucinations of a feverish mind. Just a few steps away, Durvasa sat meditating and chanting, a lotus in his hand sprinkling droplets at the end of each verse. Embarrassed that I may have violated the duties of a host, I fell back on the ground to pay respects to the saint and got up to quietly leave the room, to return in the morning when he'd need assistance. As I tiptoed out of the chamber, I heard his call from behind to sit before him. I was both scared and astonished.

You are usually asked to sit in front when you are either a rival or an equal. Disciples don't sit before their gurus, they are meant to stand behind. What was the sage thinking? Was this the beginning of some gory punishment? My feet were trembling as I came back and took position before Durvasa. For the first time in all these days, he asked me about my education! We discussed astronomy – the science behind the position of planets and the earth's gravitational pull towards the bodies in space, the cosmic radiation and the celestial observations, my understanding of planetary lords, leading to Vedic astrology. With confidence, I explained my theories and research, strangely undaunted about representing my arguments through neat diagrams. Durvasa leaned forward to understand, question, contradict and eventually stop when he was convinced. He smiled through his eyes while nodding cheerfully.

*

Almost overnight, things changed from being stressful to a smooth, breezy ride. I wrote about it in my letter to Vasudev.

'Like the slowly lifting fog on a winter morning, another human complex has been revealed. Servicing the physical needs or sharing tasks can only build the base of a relationship. Neither does it nourish the roots, nor can it secure a tough trunk to branch out from. Think about it, brother. We have seen women helping their men in lifting crops or repairing fragile constructions. We have witnessed women treating their men with great love, feeding and pleasuring their bodies, passing on gifts of progeny and building their domestic forts with dedication. Men ventured out to acquire the unseen, understand the implications and applications of geography-history-mathematics, learn archery and swordery, drive chariots and explore the world. You may argue that such a division of labour is practical. But how can the talents be matched? How would there be mutual appreciation when one half of the couple has no merit to rejoice the intelligence of the other? This arrangement leads to a shallow relationship. People are pulled towards each other to fulfil their needs but lack a deeper attachment otherwise. Their worlds aren't shared, only the bodies are. A happy relationship is the child of a spiritual union, where the intelligences of two beings communicate with each other, rising above the chores and their bodies. No misunderstanding can affect such an association; no wrath can ruin it.'

Vasudev must have laughed at my aggression.

In my conversations with Rishi Durvasa, I went deeper into the calculations of astronomy and astrology, laying down elaborate mathematical graphs. I had made many assumptions based on my study of the space, which the sage debated, corrected or accepted. Mesmerized as I was with the formation of constellations and the stars changing positions, I was equally engaged in self-driven research to decode the hierarchy–of the devas. The Vedas did analyse the position of nakshatras in correlation with their planetary gods. But that only whetted my appetite for more!

Before Durvasa, I bared all – the source and depth of all the knowledge I had gathered, most of which had not been nurtured and hence were scattered like rugged, amorphous data. Astounded that my interest had led to such an infinite extent of reading and thinking, he helped me declutter my thoughts and channelize them into a youthful flow. It felt as if he had opened a dam to welcome the abundance of a vivacious river bubbling with excitement, towards the edge and leaving freckles on the rocks. As I contemplated, the terrestrial laws started making perfect sense of everything that was scientifically claimed and rejoiced by the learned.

'Sage, I feel as though I've been promoted from a junior level of consciousness to an advanced one!'

Durvasa smiled blissfully as I urged him to guide me through more complicated calculations that could disrupt my comfort and challenge the patterns I had just learnt.

'What is it you are searching for, woman? Where are you trying to reach?' he asked affectionately.

'I wish to go back to the past of our civilization, to include in our future everything that may have got unwillingly left behind.' I wondered whether the sage had guessed the spark I had been chasing covertly.

'No one is more powerful than Time, my child. Not the devas, neither the asuras, or the humans. Unless blessed by Time itself, whoever has attempted to play with it has been mercilessly fooled. Time slips away, rendering such efforts a colossal waste.'

'I have no intention to confront Time, Rishi.' I explained as humbly as I could, to not let my confidence be perceived as arrogance. 'Aren't there three vessels of time that sail us to the multiple dimensions of an active universe? First is wisdom, second is information and the last is memories. Wisdom is the cosmic science, information is cognitive science and memory is philosophical science. I am pursuing these vessels to document the evolution.'

Pleased immensely with my response, Durvasa reached for his bag and pulled out a little *punthi*, maybe a thousand years old. I watched in awe, as the tiny document unfolded into a huge leaf, occupying almost half the room. I bent over it to carefully inspect this wonder. The sage didn't object when I touched a corner. The edge felt oily. Durvasa had inscribed on it his own research with obscure diagrams. Between his fingers he held a thin quill made from the sharpened wood of an ashoka tree. Quickly, he constructed the design of the constellations, compiling their positions and measurements across different terrestrial times, building up on the gravitational pull that the earth might have on each. He marked towards their sides, the stones on earth that were capable of capturing the energy of the planets. Accordingly, we studied the earth's access to the ruling lord of the stars. Durvasa explained, 'The spiritual bond between the elements of nature is forever transcendental. Nothing can last forever because everything in the celestial environment is constantly moving. The *nakshatra* which seems to be smiling down at us, bringing upon good fortune, will eventually move to the retrograde because such is the cosmic ploy.' Durvasa's philosophy occupied the rest of the rocky floor in geometrical blocks scribbled by him, inspiring me to think more and ask questions, provoking the sage to walk deeper into the universal truth.

Strangely, this wasn't the Durvasa who would make unusual claims at unexpected times, raising a ruckus if his volatile commands were not heeded. I had seated before me, a healer. So healing it is, when a difficult equation is resolved! Watching Durvasa engage with me in an enthusiastic pursuit of discovery, I knew the best service you can offer to a human is intellectual observation. Till the time I focused on serving him food and water dutifully, he enjoyed the favour but wasn't touched. It was only when intellectual presence was established did he notice my competence and start respecting me. The learned can only be pleasured by the resource that merits their attention. Else, the frustration of being in the company of mediocracy inflicts unpredictable behavioural fluctuations.

I had stopped feeling scared of Durvasa.

Soon it was time for the sage to leave. The farewell was unlike any other guest's after a visit. It was a very sad parting. One usually meets such a teacher only once in a lifetime. As much as I had entered the inner circle of his consciousness, equally was he overwhelmed by my yearning to explore the hidden world lurking behind the folds of earthly distractions. That morning, when Durvasa was ready to make his departure from the palace, I fell on his feet, seeking his blessings, my voice choked while bidding farewell. He placed his kind palm on my head and looked me in the eye.

'I see treasure inside you, Princess. But I am afraid these jewels might go unnoticed.' His tone was not meant to frighten, but to prepare me for the days to come. 'I was able to traverse the unbounded wealth when you had fallen ill and I attempted to pull the negative energy out of your system. Though the feeble voice was marred by pain, I heard the song of Saraswati!'

I remembered vaguely, the sage asking me to repeat some verses after him. Though I wasn't in my senses fully that evening, my subconscious had registered the ethereal attempt made by the learned man to enter the dark bottomless trench of human existence from where emerges pain and suffering.

'Princess,' I heard him say again. 'Not every human blessed with your benevolence would be deserving of your time. Yet, you wouldn't be able to cast them off, as your destiny has surrendered to the conspiracies of materialism. Life would drag you into the company of those who provoke a culture of fruitless conversations and horrid confrontations. They will prompt you to compromise on your academic engagements. I can only advise you to detach when the world seems unworthy of your brilliance, to preserve the finesse that you have built within yourself with care. Let the goddess of wisdom never be lost within layers of impositions cast by social responsibilities. Keep in touch with what you believe is really yours and discard the rest.'

I couldn't decipher the true meaning of Durvasa's words, but I could figure out he was referring to my future, inviting me to live a life of intellectual renunciation. Intelligence beyond general comprehension is never appreciated and always criticized. Instead of letting the world undeservedly dismiss my talents, the sage wanted me to withdraw and withhold. As my thoughts drifted to what kind of loneliness my quests might subject me to, Durvasa almost read my mind.

'Before I pass away from your life, royal lady, I will leave with you one last lesson. I have acquired it with great research and tremendous diligence, after starving in the wild, risking being attacked by the fierce, making peace with the dark, only to come back with a mantra. It allows me to solicit the companionship of the divine instead of waiting for the earth to fill the internal void generated by my isolation with the ignorant.'

I looked at him with great excitement. 'Is that a boon, Rishi?'

He laughed out loudly at the innocent question, shaking his head, the ribs of his body rising and falling. 'There is nothing called a boon in this world, Princess. Only knowledge and Karma. Knowledge is power. Karma decides what that knowledge does to you.' He paused and came closer. 'I will present before you a very complicated mathematical equation. You will have to crunch the numbers yourself. There would be more than one way to tame this python of a computation. The beginning will confuse you with its seven thousand heads, each more ferocious than the other. But as you manage to dive into the game, you will unlock your own progress and traverse towards the tail.'

Confused, I questioned: 'How would this mathematics battle my isolation, Rishi?'

With his voice reduced to a whisper, eyes bulging from their dark sockets and the face sparkling like a crystal, Durvasa said, 'This mantra will establish your connection with heaven and empower you to call upon the Divine. Destiny will have to step back and watch till you have pronounced your objectives and initiated your options. Your decisions would change Brahma's charts and those that are born from you would change the course of history.'

Thrilled, I sat down with Durvasa once again to take possession of this mantra. He explained a little, as does any great teacher, and refrained from helping me sail through to its solution. So delighted I was to be introduced to the magical knowledge that I failed to receive the parting words of the sage.

'Remember this, you wonderful seeker of wisdom! Great knowledge brings great responsibility. As you increasingly establish your mastery at this equation, it will tempt you to take risks and test its strength. Unless you are careful about wielding your power, it may lead to severe destruction. You should know when to restrict your curiosity. You should know how to declare your wisdom. Never stop being the princess who would put her wealth to good use instead of flaunting her fortune.'

2

The approaching month of autumn brought along bright mornings, left behind the scorching summer heat and filled the palatial gardens with seasonal blooms. Swarms of bees and butterflies performed tireless dances around the flowers, lending brightness to the brilliant vista. The large windowpanes would become the symposium for the restless little choir of birds, eager to tell more and hear less, the discourse of their daily chores. I had gone back to my usual routine of research and luxury, where I studied the world through the prism of Durvasa's teachings, while the attendants passed the smoke of camphor and jasmine on burning coconut husks through my wet hair, left hanging from the bed stand.

Vasudev came to visit us on one of those days. He seemed stronger and taller than the last time we had met. Tough muscles had started replacing the softness of his baby skin; his voice was heavier; he no longer wanted to run around the palace and, instead, started discussing politics and economics with senior ministers of the royal court, his movement brisk, body swift and demeanour confident. Unlike the dominating physical might of the Kshatriyas, his eyes had the radiance of enormous emotional intelligence. It was beyond human comprehension but something about his poise made clear that his personality was preparing to inscribe its impressions on civilization.

I watched him enter through the huge palace gates, followed by a group of attendants holding up the Yadava flag. He greeted the elders to seek their blessings; the women of the palace smeared his forehead with vermilion and sandalwood. He glanced at me strangely. In our brief exchange of words before father Kuntibhoja led him inside, he whispered to me: 'You look different; you are growing up too fast, ageing with dedication!' His wicked smile was distinctive of a teasing brother, leaving me seething behind, waiting for my opportunity to retaliate.

'What are you up to, Sister?'

That evening, I was drowned in the thoughts of Indra, staring at the vast expanse visible from the terrace. How was Indra; where was he now?

I had been exposed to a variety of texts – some prescribed by the royal professors and others, procured by my father – to rest my obstinate requisitions. I read the Rig Veda voraciously, studying again and again Indra's glorious expeditions in warfare. Ferocious, sharp and invincible. Durvasa's mathematical challenge had just cleared a layer of smog that hid my path to the king of the devas yet planted a colossal gate with tenacious locks at the entrance. Hasn't the obscure always tempted the seeker to destroy the intermediary barriers? I was deeply absorbed within the clots of the equation when my brother's voice boomed from behind and I turned.

'Where had you been all through the day?' I asked with angst. This time my brother had not created the ruckus in my chamber that was once his delightful pastime and my favourite pain. His sudden maturity had become an impolite threat to our spontaneous friendship! He didn't need me as much anymore. He had taken the flight to engage with the other world that lay distanced from me, owing to its dust and gullibility, making himself available to the uncouth. He spent his youthful time with our subjects – the peasants and merchants and cleaners!

Vasudev didn't understand his sister's complaints.

Looking around, he said: 'Sister, though you were bred in an ambiance of affluence, you have served a sage, lately, with great loyalty. But I must tell you, neither the penance of the sage, nor the opulence of this palace represents the life of the majority in this kingdom. I am tasked to learn from the common people in diverse corners, so I can serve them well as a leader, later.' He smiled, enraging me more. I turned away. With great affection, he stood in front of me, diluting my displeasure. I frowned at him but couldn't hold my resentment for too long.

The sounds of the holy bell from the royal temple reverberated all through the town, symbolic of the passing time that would stop for none. Peasants of the country were busy observing their seeds, traders were counting the collections against daily targets, the priest was finishing his classes after the students had diligently chanted shlokas from the Isha Upanishad. Just beyond the orchard in the northwest, the army chief had built a rough bed of dry mud and sand for soldiers to practise wrestling and sword fights. Their screams of exhilaration travelled through the thin air. I could see them through the mesh of trees. I twitched under my breath. The moves of fighters needed to be more unpredictable.

Everyone was engaged in furthering the functions they had come to the earth for, yet standing before me was the candescence of humanity! A strange glow that I couldn't trace was emanating from Vasudev. It was mesmerizing.

What had changed so much in him? Was it the usual effect of time that had blessed his strength with the lordly grace? I couldn't interpret the source of the change and it left me severely restless, until I saw my brother smiling through his eyes.

'You think too much,' he suggested.

Forgetting all insinuations, my palm touching his cheek and hair, I blurted out, 'What is it I see in you, which I hadn't before?'

'The sixth sense,' he explained, confusing me more. 'You are a seeker of the outer self, dear sister, in thrall to the beauty of vision, audio, smell, taste and touch. My pursuit is the knowledge of the inner self. I experience its response growing within my system, enriching the soul with the warmth of the divine.' He waited to figure out how clearly I was comprehending his claims. Truth be admitted, I didn't really understand. Vasudev seemed distant, far ahead from my intelligence and yet strangely connected! He was letting slip some secrets, most of which I would struggle to decipher. With a loving smile, he added, 'Sister, I feel God in me.'

A divine domination deep inside was getting increasingly powerful with each passing day, enhancing his patience, resilience and humility, Vasudev explained. Not that I had grasped it completely, but I could see it manifesting through my brother's wisdom and peace. He looked like the sole being in an enormous world of his own, cut off from everyone else around and yet in touch to fulfil all duties. He would listen more and talk seldom. The restless brother I had once known was now determined to conserve his energy! And he had a clear instinct for the future!

'My intuition says, dear sister, that you will amass the best return of the five indriyas bestowed upon us. The five senses will form an indomitable construct, for which you will be envied by many, but defeated by none. And my future will foresee a similar construct, in submission to the invincible sixth sense.'

'What more, Brother?' I asked, trying to analyse Vasudev's words with deft sincerity, wondering if human intuition can be as specific as the science of astrology. He smiled. 'Your future will acquire the power that will see clearer, hear deeper and feel more distinctly than any other human. It will be the amalgamation of positive senses with intense social intelligence. But great power will bring great vulnerability. My strength with its emotional intelligence, will protect yours like a guiding angel. It will offer clarity to profound algorithms and demystify human clutter with better coherence than my illustrations here, on this evening.'

We waited in silence, as the daylight slid behind dusk. The twilight layers spread a tranquil linen over the agile world but couldn't mellow the brightness in front. His energy glowed in the darkness.

'I can tell you this with confidence that this evening will repeat itself, when my future will impart larger life lessons to yours. It would be a starkly different situation where mankind will face the most horrifying dilemma threatening to uproot every virtue they had acquired all through their existence.'

Astounded as I was with Vasudev's vision, I couldn't refute his predictions. I had seen glimpses of them when I sat engrossed with my astrological charts, calculating the interplay of time and planets, to comprehend the language of Karma. I saw myself trapped in the wild, I saw fire. I saw a visually impaired chief. I heard the melodious resounding of rhythmic tools obsessed with creation. A magical architect was constructing *maya nagari* – a palace that could confuse the corrupt. I heard the laughter of the devil sitting with a destructive dice. I saw a woman, from behind – her open, unkempt hair symbolizing great insult, her dark skin shamelessly exposed, red fist of the right hand holding the blood-stained *kharga* of Mahakali – walking ahead to rack up massive disaster, her feet soaked in vengeance. I saw a catastrophic war.

There were voices from the future, one depressed with his standing in life, the other explaining the records of Karma. One was trapped in his own metaphysical ignorance, the other was determined to pull him out of that *avidya*, releasing him from the misconception of self and upgrading to the consciousness of the divine.

Briefly, I got a peek into some indistinct image of an old man asking a small boy, amid many others, 'What do you see in front?'

An arrow held on to his bow, his arms straight and spine erect, his bare torso held the luminance of a thousand warriors. 'I see nothing but the bird's eye, Gurudev,' the thin voice retorted.

'You may proceed,' the command echoed. The arrow left the bow with great dexterity, piercing through the air and brought the poor bird down. I caught a glimpse of the face that belonged to the thin voice. The one who hears what no one else can, sees what is required with acute concentration, tastes all elements of life from the basic to the magnificent, smells the advancing danger and touches like a forlorn lover.

My son with Indra!

3

That morning, before even the birds had started chirruping, I sat studying the designs left behind by Durvasa. The sage had left for good but the Ishan griha had woken up from his brilliance, unwilling to fall back into its passive slumber in the isolated corner of the palace. Towards the entrance, a torch burned unextinguished, the wall or its rocky cast gathering no tar. Visible from my bedside window was its metallic base below the dancing fire, pulsating hypnotically. I was plucked away from the bejewelled designs of the soft bed to the concrete sleepless floors that provoked discoveries. The rays of the sun entered here first, every morning, as if in acknowledgement of the energy that stayed back even after the sage had gone. I spread the calculations on the ground, after feeding fuel to the fidgety lamp in the corner. It was indeed an enormous puzzle, breeding a mesh of thorns from seven different directions. The more difficult it seemed, the stronger grew my resolution to tame the monstrous numbers.

With his parting advice during the last visit, Vasudev had assured me, 'Never believe what you seek isn't worth seeking. Because it's your faith if not his will, that will bring him to you as a captive to your needs.'

'What do you know about this *him*?' I had asked, and Vasudev laughed.

'Nothing, just a personification of your goals, maybe. The merit that you consider an equal!'

I didn't ask more.

I had crossed several stages of this mathematical model and was yet to penetrate through a few more. This stage calls upon a state of dissolution when one feels stuck sometimes. The brain feels too clotted and yet, there's no stopping even momentarily, because fresh possibilities keep churning inside the curious mind. At each stage, the computation kept teasing my abilities, burning the ego with infinite roadblocks when a partial calculation would go wrong. I had left my food to return to the task. While absorbing new lessons from the royal professors, my attention had deviated. Even my father's gifts of silk and gold couldn't hold my loyalty. The final gate of mathematics had impeded my ingress with a strange lock. It had tested my patience enough and I moved with caution. I proceeded restlessly and was thwarted every time, having to begin the stage again from scratch. Frustrated to the hilt and proffered a fire test for tolerance, I sweated profusely. My nerves throbbed, as did the muscles of men outside, trying to train a wild elephant. I was tired but not ready to give up until I had reached the end. That was when I was prompted to seek blessings from the power I connected with. It acted as the final password. Taken aback, I looked up. Exhausted eyes touched the morning sun through the wall-sized window. It was dawn already, time for me to worship the sun god – the ritual I had been taught by Rishi Durvasa.

'Surya is the embodiment of knowledge,' he would say. 'Your competence in astrology, the ability to see the past and the future, the urge to know more, learn more, understand more is blessed by his light. He would shine for you when all is dark. Cherish the privileges, pamper the power.' The sage would raise his hands over his head and bring the joined palms down to his chest with deep regards. Habituated to the morning custom now, I took a short break from the giant riddle, raised my hands and brought them down to my chest. The sun looked resplendent with orange and purple streaked across the blue. Pleasant rays presented nature in its youth – life on earth smiling back to the brightness, energized to pass through their exhaustive chores once again with vigour. This energy touched me back. I closed my eyes to concentrate, inviting the eternal shine to bless my diligence.

I uttered the chants quickly and went back. Fatigued with days of studying numbers, I didn't wish to delay this stage, now that it seemed almost in my grasp. But something had gone terribly amiss! Nerves stiffened, my fingers closed into a fist. The equations suddenly seemed no longer in my control. They had started compiling by themselves, the numbers bonding and releasing by some strange automation, facilitating decisions on my behalf.

Life is the biggest ploy of mathematics. Two fallen on five invariably makes it seven. The next level must begin from the sum and not from the contributing digits. Couldn't things be more flexible in the core survival models?

In haste and impatience, I had made the most pernicious error in my understanding of the mystery of calculations! Irredeemable now.

A sudden hush fell on the earth. Even though my eyes were wide open, the world around me blurred. I was travelling, but I didn't know the destination. The only audible sound was the strange buzz of an invisible spaceship that I hadn't summoned. By the time the droning sound faded away and my eyes could touch stationary objects again, I had already been transported to some other land. This wasn't bordered by barbed walls or protective doors. It seemed to be an open secret waiting to be surveyed. A blast of light did not hurt the eyes but was smooth enough to pleasure and glossy enough to charm. Everything here seemed to be touched by raw gold. Very dark nights can impair your sight, and so can unexpected brightness. I used my palms to form a shade. The few trees standing on the sides looked a hundred thousand years old, their branches crooked, trunks feeble and leaves mostly decayed brown between the greens. The fallen leaves travelled with the breeze following strange patterns, covering the dusty path before me, as if offering a special welcome. I stepped on them and they cracked. I was not aware of this show of nature – rugged and indigenous, with a spirit of its own. In my father's kingdom, I had always had the luxury of a carrier with silk curtains, so the dust wouldn't touch my skin. That was before Durvasa let loose a stream of daunting tasks, which made me run from one direction to another, heedless of what I was stepping on or cutting through. This day as the dry leaves tickled my skin and ruptured below the feet, I felt nature in its most spontaneous splendour. Amused, I laughed. The vibrations echoed through the wind, binding the pitch into an invisible casket and carrying it like treasure for some invisible monarch. Along the sides of the golden meadows interspersed with blonde ingrowths, stood gigantic, isolated structures overlooking the sea of orange waves. Unsure of my destination, I walked through the deserted nature towards the reclusive edifice, hoping to find some humanly presence behind their doors.

As I moved ahead, the structures got clearer. I could now see a tall castle clung upon by the clouds towards the top. There was no gate at the entrance but a huge round bordered by the designs of a chariot wheel. In order to enter the premises and explore further, I would have to turn this wheel. I looked around suspiciously. Other than the withered trees, not a single being was breathing. Hesitation coupled with curiosity,

I peeped inside. It looked dark, steep and desolate, as if I'd fall into a deep trench if I took a step further. Why was I here? And what lay beyond the turn of the wheel?

My head warned me against proceeding.

'A Kshatriya can't succumb to fear. I need to know what the mantra has brought me to.' The heart countered.

Eyes closed in denial of the step I was taking, I turned the wheel and took the leap. I didn't fall into the chasm. I couldn't feel the ground below my feet, but I was still standing erect by some unexplained power. Slowly, I opened my eyes and looked around. It wasn't as dark inside as it had seemed. This space had no roof. I looked up, my eyes reached the unbarred infinite. What a weird esoteric suspension!

The sight before me was exquisite. Ripples of the ocean below changed colours from turquoise to indigo. Deep orange penetrated through them by the delightful intervention of some enchanting wizard. Flickers of golden glitters floated around in the air. They stuck to my palm by some mischievous adhesives, every time I tried to touch them. All control slipping out of my spinning head, I tried to stop myself from thinking more. A dense, fluttery, invisible curtain was dissolving into thin air to introduce the space, soft clouds floating around and birds chirping far beneath. The sight in front soon became distinct; my eyes came together in bewilderment. I could see the kingdom of Kuntibhoja many nakshatras away, the royal courtyard where my childhood hours were spent reciting verses prompted by the palace professors. I saw the Ishan griha, few floors above where I sat chanting the mantra. In another direction, I saw the kingdom of Hastinapur. I had never been there but who on earth had not known the great prince Devavrat, now called Bhishma because of his impossible vow of celibacy and sacrifice for the throne! Who thought that a warrior could possess such might to protect his father's heart? No more than a few miles away from Hastinapur, a celestial architect was constructing the magical city of Indraprastha! The sound of his hammer and anvil seemed to rhyme with the missing beats of my heart. What was my connection with this future city called Indraprastha? Why this name? I inched closer, keen eyes attending to this vision with immense concentration. This architect was Mayasur, thrusted with the task of erecting an imperial court.

Was that Indra's home with me on earth? I couldn't take my eyes off it.

Before I could immerse further into an ambitious future of holding the Devraj captive within the folds of my cloth, earthly glimpses flamed through the dreamy camaraderie with the divine. Further north, the frames of a burning house in Varnavrat touched the sky. Monstrous laughter of the conspirators celebrated vicious victory but were soon disillusioned with the realization that their victims were unscathed. Princes of the great dynasty, fathered by the visually impaired, were blind enough to the obligations that befall a Kshatriya upbringing. They set their path towards lawlessness, misusing every learning they were fortunate to behold.

In the devastating war that was to follow, I saw my blood on either side of Dharma!

*

But why should I see these now? Why here? And then it dawned. Had I entered the outhouse of Surya?

Feeling worried, I rushed back to locate the rounded hole through which I had entered. It was no longer visible. I ran hither and thither restlessly, throwing my hands into the air, expecting to hit the edge of the entrance. But the structure had vanished!

'Is anyone there? Can you help? I have lost my way!' I screamed.

The sound waved southwards towards the sea and lost its influence to the infinite. Sceptically, I looked at it. The vast orange spread wasn't the sea of water. Voices bubbled there, chaotic but faintly audible – hymns in praise of the sun god or earnest pleas demanding his attention – from the past and the future, from the young and the old, from humans and animals and insects, from worlds I didn't even know existed. Resigned, I waited to face whatever was to follow.

I was now supposed to be with the royal priest in the palace temple.

'The *navagrah* or the nine astronomical bodies as per Vedic astrology, are the relay stations for the reception and transmission of stellar energies,' he told me once, during his lessons. 'These are Sun, Moon, Mars, Mercury, Jupiter, Venus and Saturn, representing the seven days of the week, along with the shadowy planets, Rahu and Ketu. Leading the navagrah is the sun, ruling over our consciousness and intelligence, exalting wisdom and censoring the inner child within humans, empowering them to reason things out with their analytical ability. The sun is our basic identity, representing self-realization. Sun is the psychology which dominates our actions. We think, dream, imagine, float and falter amid a thousand desires, driven by the moon and other planets, but ultimately, it is the sun that decides our reality.'

These words had felt profound when I heard them for the first time. Now they seemed shallow. The old man must be getting restless, wondering why I hadn't reached on time. Soon, father Kuntibhoja would be informed that his daughter had gone missing. Would they realize I had been taken hostage by Surya? What had I landed myself in? I covered my face with my palms, trying to hatch an escape strategy.

A voice from behind made me turn. 'Welcome to Surya's abode, elegant princess.'

The peaceful eyes of the sun god and his glistening skin extended a pristine welcome. Unsure of whether the god was just being courteous before pronouncing a punishment in response to my intrusion, I took a few steps back. He didn't seem offended. Finally, there was hope. I would have to convince him to let me go. Surya had a pleasant smile pasted on his lips. It would be a peace treaty, not a conflict.

'Apologies for having entered your chamber by mistake,' I regretted. 'I don't know how to help myself out, so I don't prolong the interruption.'

Bewildered, Surya stared at me for a short while and eventually broke into a gentle laughter, cornering me more with the confusion.

'You haven't chanced through my doors, princess. No mortal can do that, unless decreed by elevated capabilities,' he explained calmly. 'You have entered this space because you were meant to. You chose my palace long before you understood the meaning of making a choice. Your love for knowledge affiliates your being as one of the elite stakeholders within my federation. You are married to my ideals by virtue of your intelligence.'

Jolted by Surya's claim, I stared dumbfounded, my feet rooted to the spot. How could I belong to Surya? Hadn't I always longed for Indra, ever since I had understood the meaning of love? Hadn't I given myself to the Devraj through elaborate rituals and academic texts and fantasized about him being my lover? Didn't I prepare myself with all my might, seeking the mightiest to hold me in his arms, reciprocating the passion in acknowledgement of my submission? How can the devotee of Indra invite the attention of Surya? Could any of my actions have been misinterpreted as such a sinful digression? I wanted to leave and never look back.

The observer of all saw me shuddering. He let out a deep breath and turned to look in front, where my window was visible, afar.

'Before you, Princess, lies the *brahmanda*, the universe. From these chambers, you can see through time. You got to see your kingdom with clarity. You could also see your future. The kingdom of Hastinapura and the fate of warring families. Such is my light that touches all and hides nothing.' He looked at me with affection. 'In your quests, you had attracted my intimacy as your legitimate companion. On this auspicious day, when you have cracked the most difficult codes of the divine mantra, you were led to my chambers by the design of Karma, though you may call it a novice error of mismatched action.' He paused.

My awareness raised to comprehend Surya's arguments and yet, stubbornly refuting them all, I held my ground with an honest confession. 'I am in love with Indra!'

'And Surya is in love with you, Princess.' the sun god declared, his features shining with the mirth of a confident lover, immune to the mention of another man before him. Bathed in an invincible quest for Indra, I may have underrated Surya's patience. The cosmos was experiencing this strange adjournment for the first time. A woman loyal to another lover had sinfully stepped inside someone else's private chambers! How, I didn't know. Why, I didn't want to know. But Surya seemed to be at the loss of nothing, not even self-glory, at my unwavering resolve.

'I am not unaware of your desires.' I heard him saying. 'You are a complex woman with stark contradictions.'

'Falling in love is no contradiction, Deva. I admit I may have been ambitious. But I believe that I deserve whom I desire,' I tried to reason, perplexed by anyone doubting my qualifications to love Indra.

'You have been a seeker of truth. I am that truth, presenting before you the world in its untarnished worth. And yet, while your intelligence appreciates accuracy, you have given yourself to the love for the illusion. Indra is a magnificent illusion. If this isn't contradiction, what else is?' Surya voice beamed through the universe, his words touched mountains and oceans and deserts. Alas, it couldn't touch a woman's heart.

'Your conscious choices define your dreams, your subconscious interests reveal your character.' He philosophized.

I felt my nerves and veins revolting to Surya's explanations. They were too obnoxious to accept; the reality that attempts to displace the confidence.

'No, Deva.' I objected stubbornly. 'My conscious and my subconscious, my dreams and my character, have all always known only one form of devotion. For the rest, not every fondness is desire.'

'You haven't been sent here to fall in love Princess.' his voice was sombre now. 'But every journey entails a payback to the one you owe the most. At this moment, you are to face that choice, whether you offer homage or discard the lover destined to nourish you, for the one you have never seen.'

Taken aback by the ruthless ultimatum, I wondered what kind of man would still adore the woman who nurtures in her heart such desire for another being.

'Why must I be placed before such a crossroad, Deva?' The question slipped out of my mouth.

'Because truth and illusion cannot exist together. They are the two opposite sides of the spectrum. When Indra brings rains, Surya must be clouded. When Surya is in power, the clouds retreat.' Surya explained, perhaps with great restraint from his will to leave me stranded with my confusions. He could speak the most bitter truth with an informal detachment.

The conversation was a foreshadowing of the gory times when Surya's son and Indra's son would become stark enemies, thirsting for each other's blood. At that hour, I was too occupied by my predicament to understand those signals. Before I could utter a word, he said, 'But, you may have the power to look through the illusion and embrace its truth. Indra will draw you into his majestic world, marking your future with the valour of a skilful warrior. Your union with me will cast the perfect world with many complications, as does every wise individual's, when faced with the inherent battle against mediocrity; however, my faculty will bless you with divine intelligence that cannot be enveloped by illusion. Whether you welcome this relationship or reject this alliance is a decision I leave with you.'

No words could communicate the dilemma that was churning inside my mind. Insulted by my silence, Surya left the spot in broad steps. The energetic brightness followed him, leaving behind a grim luminance. Relieved by his departure and yet laden with guilt, my knees gave way.

4

'Sage, what world have you thrown me to?' I accused Durvasa. 'Why do I deserve to be Surya's prisoner?'

There was no answer. Life was visible, many stars away; here it was an obnoxious confinement. An inner voice piped up in defence of Durvasa.

'You are a captive of your own obstructions. Surya didn't call you here. It's you who turned every wheel, curiously or unintentionally.'

'Just tell me the way out.' I wanted to scream. With a restless restraint, I pressed my fingers into my temples. I got up to look for the giant wheel again; it was nowhere. I tried to hit upon something. Even that privilege was confiscated.

After cracking one monstrous riddle, I had rewarded myself by entering another and this time, it would suffocate me till death.

I closed my eyes. It was lifelessly quiet here, yet the melody of a soft hum was unmissable. Slowly, the hum grew louder and the melody gave in to uncomfortable noises. I turned towards the west. The sea of prayers was getting tumultuous. Waves piled on, slamming against one another. Voices – energetic and retired, timid and shrill – were trying to override each other in a frenzy. High tides brought by enormous miseries threatened to engulf the universe. Raising their head through the vehicles of complaints were also the chants of mankind, singing praises for the benevolence of the sun god. Laces of gratitude frothed through the wails for mercy. Though afar, the waves seemed to cross their boundaries and flood forward. Were they coming towards me? I stepped back.

'Set him free, sinful woman!' I heard the menacing waves attempting to choke me with their allegations.

'Set whom free?' I uttered in shock.

'Our god. The benefactor of light. We have crops to grow. We have transactions pending. How dare you cast such profanity upon the world? How could you have your impious spell enveloping the sun god to such inactivity?'

Taken aback by such an insinuation, I wondered how to convince the angry waves it was I who was suffering the imprisonment. Not Surya. But my experience in closely observing people and politics had taught me that arguments with angry mobs didn't lead to favourable solutions. I had to find a way out.

The head felt like a dishevelled city ransacked by devastating fire. From which end do I start the restoration? I looked in the direction of Hastinapur again. There I was travelling along, dressed in pristine white, bereft of the vermilion, walking alone in the dark, followed silently by Vidur, the other face of Dharma – a descendant of the sun god. The restlessness turned into cold shivers as I saw myself as a youthful widow.

Me, a widow!

The kingdom with the glory of great warriors was being devastated by the guile. The goodness of my illustrious sons interpreted as weakness by the foolish, would lead to unthinkable hardships, until the invincible be vanquished by their own arrogance. Life would force me to battle many deceits that conspire perilous attempts to counter my observation and harm my children. In the days to come, my intelligence would be my biggest armour.

I don't know for how long I watched them, but in that phase of self-absorption, a lot of muddled visions started falling into a pattern. It wouldn't be wise to provoke Surya's ire. Having him as an ally could be highly valuable, later. Else who can predict when politics would seek unpredictable favours?

'Calm down, woman. Surya isn't a destroyer.' I tried to convince myself. 'He is the sacrificial fire that refines. The union with Light will have its consequences; but it might bestow the foresight against all perils that attempt to demean you, threatening the most enterprising wait for your love.'

'What will I tell Indra, whenever I do?' my heart murmured sadly, trying to hide the crime even before it was committed.

'Did Indra seek your loyalty?' the head laughed, pushing the heart towards non-existence. 'Are you born to be an idol of sacrifice, foolish enough to miss out the opportunities?'

Startled now, I sat up. 'What opportunities?'

'Surya wouldn't impress with the fragrance of petals; he'd attract with neither riches nor glorifications. The sun god isn't capable of showering the fervent feeling of love. He shows unadulterated pictures from the present, past and future, disabling the confinements of wishful assumptions. Surya is the window of truth; that is the only expression he knows. And you are smarter than a woman in distress.'

This time, the heart raised no further objections.

I walked with bold steps through the same corridors Surya had left behind, to enter the interiors of a private sphere. He sat there resigned, looking neither pained, nor resentful. The divine illumination was inspiring. I mustered all the courage to be empowered by this radiance.

Surya turned with a smile. 'What have you come to negotiate, princess?'

I faltered, looking baffled. Surya did not praise my body, sang no ballads in praise of my beauty. His love didn't seek to possess. He was at peace with his own vastness, not to be dwarfed by limitations of others. Before I made myself heard, Surya spoke again.

'The mantra that brought you here is a liberation as much as it is a trap, wonderful woman.' He exhaled a deep breath that seemed to shake the universe. 'It mandates you and me to give ourselves to each other. The scope of choice you left behind, when you cracked the last leg of the codes.' The burden was displeasing but Surya didn't complain. He did look thoughtful, though. 'You and I cannot leave these chambers till we fulfil the dictate of the mantra. Until then, the exit will remain sealed. And if I am not relieved from this obligation within stipulated hours, another part of the world will never see daylight.'

'How can I be blamed for keeping you away, Deva?' I tried to reason. 'The truth is –'

'The truth is not what you see. Your feeling of being hoodwinked is not the truth.' Resigned, I waited for the god to explain himself. He did.

'We are part of this vast system called the universe. The planets are the sources of divine energy. Everything and everyone is on an evolutionary journey under the influence of these energies. The elements of the solar system are systematic but ever-moving.' I stood calmly listening to him, my attention wavering frequently and coming back again.

'All chemical reactions on the earth are a result of that constant motion.' Surya sighed deeply. 'The people from the earth cannot spend time in heaven, with their earthly consciousness. Until anyone is deported to be brought back again, the world stops functioning, which results in a cosmic imbalance. Life halts.'

This time, I was shaken. The sea of prayers was invisible from Surya's hidden chamber, but the uproar was audible. The waves were growing rowdy with each wasted moment, lashing upon each other, searching for Surya, blaming a youthful enchantress for bewitching him.

Wide-eyed, I asked the obvious. 'How would my entry to Surya's land impact the earthlings?'

'All blessings are a hidden curse and all curses are a hidden blessing ...' he paused. 'While the earth would be blessed with life-altering consequences from your visit to heaven as a living human, both you and I would equally have to bear the punishments for our sinful intervention with time! The more you delay your stay, our sins multiply. Set me free, Princess, and yourself, too.' Profound grief reflected ruthlessly in the words of the one who didn't know how to hide it.

'When you are cornered by the inevitable, the inevitable becomes your Dharma.' Vasudev's advice last summer loomed inside my head. 'Not every time, dear sister, will you be permitted by your conscience to think as an individual. You are a Kshatriya. Life will demand courage from you to put aside your wishes and abide by your Dharma.

Such decisions could be difficult, but they will indelibly writ your legacy in history.' Did Vasudev know I was to face such a dilemma, wherein I would be professed love by the benevolent, forcing me to debate whether the Dharma of a princess overshadowed the desire of a woman?

'Think before you act.' Vasudev's voice floated back again. 'The twists and turns of life are indefinite and endless; sometimes disastrous, but inevitable nevertheless.'

I would have to stop thinking as an individual and start thinking like a princess. There lies the freedom, I decided.

'Fine then.' I told myself. 'If I must step over Surya to set the cosmos back in motion, then so be it.'

I clenched my teeth so hard onto my lower lip, it bled. I walked forward and touched Surya. With empathy and kindness, Surya wiped the stains of blood off my lips with his fingers. His touch, warm and mild, dried the blood immediately. He passed his fingers through my hair. I was immediately pulled into an inordinate flash of light where the sun god held me by the waist, my hands clasping his shoulders, nails digging into his skin, eyes closed and hair flowing behind. We were soon cocooned into a cluster of clouds when I felt Surya's lips on the skin below my neck. A flash of heat ran through my pulse, exploding the turmoil of my own body. As we unrobed each other, Surya with enormous patience and I, with the excitement of discovery, celestial note-keepers documented the texts of the future with enormous speed. The future that would bring me to Surya again and again, with regrets and remorse, in silence and disquiet, though for the ignorant world, my courage and regality would shine eternally like illustrious daylight.

When Surya entered the forbidden domains of femininity, I closed in on him to take all that he had to give. The closeness brought a faraway vision from the times when I would be greying, my eyes still sparkling but body failing to catch up with the energy of the mind. I found myself explaining life to another woman kneeling before me, her hair untied and messy, which I tried my best to oil and place back into ordered strands. As much as I attempted to coil them into a neat braid, they would fall apart. The oil did nothing to nourish her overt growth. The strands demanded blood!

I wanted to turn her face towards me and see who she was, to whom I was making so many tiring confessions at the fag end of my existence. What made me answerable to her? But Surya's energy had already found its release; his light was fading on me now. It was too pale to reach so many years into the future.

We rose to our feet as it was time to bid goodbye. We were free from the binding spell now. We stared at each other till Surya chose to turn away first, taking fast steps out to calm the stormy sea of prayers. The wheel for exit was visible again on the other end. I walked towards it with stern steps, trying to tell myself that this day wouldn't matter; this hour wouldn't be revisited and I wouldn't need Surya ever again. A drop of tear rebelled down; I wiped it quickly.

*

Tears shamed my skin, as I watched Surya from the window at Kuntibhoja's palace. A beautiful red ball of orange with a tinge of purple and yellow. Indigo and scarlet spread through the foamy clouds over the vast expanse of the sky. This was meant to be an evening of celebration. Seven colours of the sun mingled with each other to procure more hues than the canopy downstairs. Black, brown and white horses parked on the graze-yard with representative flags flying high to introduce the energies and honour of their owners. Flavours from the kitchen raked up even the recluse, inviting mongrels and humans alike, to grace the open invitation of the majestic ceremony. Thick garlands of marigold and jasmine enwrapped the royal pillars, their fragrance reaching every subject of the kingdom. They discussed the handsome suitors who had gathered at our palace to participate in the *swayamvar* of their beloved princess.

The attendants combed my hair, passed the fragrant smoke of camphor through it, curled it up into an elaborate bun and embellished it with colourful flowers. The red of my wedding trousseau had rich golden embroidery on the finest of threads. Thick ornaments gripped my neck, my ears, my hands, waist and feet. I had acquired the beauty of a thousand nymphs. Or so they said. Yet, the world seemed pale.

Indra hadn't arrived.

5

Indra is the fierce warrior that saved the earth by slaying the demons, Vala and Vritra, who had blocked water and aimed to destroy the peace and happiness among humans. Riding his chariot and wielding a thunderbolt popularly called *vajra,* Indra released the water with incredible valour, gaining control over the skies to bring forth thunder and rainfall.

I have read these descriptions many times, fantasizing my seat on the lord's six-trunked white elephant Airavat, supervising the unpredictable elements of space with Indra himself seated on Uchchaihshravas, his invincible seven-headed horse, introducing me to his secret estates as we rode together, hand in hand.

'Why did you want me, Kunti?' he asked in my dreams.

'I am Kunti, the princess,' I would erupt. 'I am inaccessible to the ordinary, Deva. The inferior cannot match up to my brilliance; their touch doesn't merit my acumen. The king that stands before me will not be constrained within the limitations of a kingdom fenced by the human. I deserve to be wedded to the king of the devas.' The pride filled my face with a bold, astute smile. I could foresee the enthusiastic prediction as if it were being played before me. My feminine intelligence would engage with Indra's masculine vigour, birthing an indomitable force that employs both body and mind in securing, strengthening and defeating. My union with Indra will also bestow upon my progeny, the deva's gift of illusions, potent enough to inspire love and lethal enough to trap the opponent within its masquerading grandeur. The seeker of truth would be armed with the art of manipulating it and displaying that magic on the battlefield. The royal storage would overflow, rivals would take a bow. Trade and growth would expand along with the swelling national boundaries.

I would mother nothing less than an indestructible, dauntless legacy!

When it rained last monsoon, I had rushed out to the open plains of the valley, seeking Indra to respond to my calls. Layered clouds crowded in, monopolizing the ecosphere with full-blown trumpets. From behind the hillocks, a feathery haze ran sidewards. People wrapped up their pending work and rushed home. Plants swayed in delight, birds flapped their wings sending ripples in the lakes, fawns raced in herds, peacocks mated. Such a gathering of nature is the inkling of an angelic arrival. A drop of water from above tickled the eyelashes. I chuckled. Soon, the valley was drenched with the abundance of monsoon. With great patience, I waited for hours till nature relaxed and the last drop of the rains mocked on my forehead. Wandering alone in the terrains, I broke into angry tears. The drying teaks on both sides of the valley had just been infused with fresh life. Their scornful murmurs made scandalous gossips for the passing winds.

'Did you notice the audacity of the mortal? The earth-born claims to love the king of the devas and got generously flouted.' One grimaced.

'Who says a dwarf isn't permitted to have tall dreams?' Said another and they broke into cruel laughter.

Hurt tremendously by Indra's negligence, more than the banters of the uncouth, I moved on. I had fantasized him approaching me as a lover, starved to receive the bounteous touch that differentiates the majestic from the mundane. But neither longing, nor sophistication had been able to convince the divine lover of my merits. The cold air pricked my skin through the wet clothes. Offended and abused thus by the curt rejection, I fell on the slippery surface, my skin burning and throat heavy with a lump.

The sun was shining in glory now, the rays wrapped me in a comfortable sheet. The warmth cleansed my tear-flushed face. I picked up my tired self and walked back towards the palace.

Late that night, the monsoon visited again.

Seated on the bedside window, I called out more assertively. Like a friend I spread my hands and played with the downpour, allowing it to touch at times and withdrawing suddenly when it found me easily. We both laughed. The monsoon raised its melody, falling upon the leaves and the soil like the bow on a violin. I tried to match the tunes, my harsh endeavours abruptly discordant. We laughed again, but I didn't stop singing. The talent, embarrassed immensely by an unequal, begged for me to stop. I gently passed a furtive condition. 'Tell me about Indra, my beautiful companion.'

Unsuspectingly, she asked, 'What do you wish to know, wonderful?'

'I want to see his spread, hear his voice, smell his identity, touch his body and taste his power.' I said with excitement. 'I want to experience him in tangible terms. I want the deva to acknowledge me. He cannot appear stealthily in the dark and flee by daylight; he would have to own me and be owned, as deserves the pride of a princess.'

My words made the rains laugh amid bouts of thunder. The sizzling downpour got mischievous, changing directions and coming back to its place.

'Princess, in your obsession to own Indra, you have lost the realization of Indra. You will experience him when you wouldn't bind him with obligations. He resides in elements more than a form. You will find him in the wilderness of nature, in the eloquence of poetry, in the clanging of swords. Boundless and free of shackles. He is around you now, but you can't feel him!' The rains twirled around, raising the sweet smell of moist soil, and danced to its own melody. I tried to get hold of it; only some droplets remained on my palm, the rest slipped away.

'Where is Indra now?' I asked in exasperation.

'Look at yourself and everything around you.' The downpour whispered like a celestial nymph. 'His vajra is symbolic of human nature, reinforcing courage and strength when it is required most. The lightning bolt is symbolic of the spiritual energy lying dormant within hearts. When used in context, it can translate into great power.'

'Isn't Indra an indulgent lover?' I argued back.

'Yes, he is.' The friend lowered her voice more, passing confidential information. 'The spiritual energy representing his vajra comes from his women. Just like sufferers seek support of Indra before every vicious war, Indra approaches the feminine energy to recharge himself for warfare. That feminine energy, he wins over with love or seizes with passion.'

'Isn't love supposed to be selfless?' the innocent question escaped my mouth.

'Not every love is selfless.' Chuckles of the rain jingled like my foot ornaments. I sank into silence. 'Indra's love cannot be selfless. He has greater responsibilities. He has to protect the Devalaya, which is prone to attacks from Asuras and from over-ambitious sages who are hungry to gain control over heaven. The king has political priorities.'

'All with the strength of the feminine energy?' I was bewildered.

The rumble of rains echoed from all sides. 'Have you heard about *soma*, Princess?' It rustled. 'Soma is an intoxicating plant that causes hallucinations. It is also available in feminine nature. Indra resorts to illusions empowered by the *rasa*, as his intelligence in warfare accentuates.'

The water came lashing down, isolating me from the verbose. So this was Indra's secret? His affinity for the soma? My eyes narrowed. The mankind and the Asura stay fooled with the impression that the soma rasa that enhances Indra's strength comes from a plant. Only the wise would know that Indra's secret to the rasa lies in his intimacy with concubines!

'Women are another face of maya,' the rains asserted. 'Their tenderness evokes warmth, their grace is subliminal. Indra unites with women to partner with their courage and intellect, available in abundance amid nature, but the women know better about trapping those elements floating like remote particles and organizing them in patterns to be retrieved when required. The woman remains calm under pressure. She invokes compassion, being the emotional anchor of a community. No structure can survive without the feminine foundation. Indra derives his qualifications to rule over Indraloka from the spirit of bonding, networking and creativity of diverse feminine forces. Indra's alliance with women is more diplomatic than personal, a collaboration over companionship.'

*

That evening, the rains professed, Indra would be available when I would have travelled enough, making my way through the manipulations of life, when my soul would have accumulated enough soma. But he wouldn't ever marry me. Devas can't wed the mortals. Despite understanding, I did expect Indra to come and dismantle this debacle called the swayamvar. The tall chariots and energetic horses bedecked with gold meant nothing to me if one of them wasn't Uchchaihshravas. I nurtured a hopeless dream in the bleak, for Indra to come riding in speed, raising dust storms, to pick me up by the waist and disappear within the clouds. When Vasudev held my hand and ushered me towards the canopy downstairs, all my fantasies crashed like broken pieces of glass. I walked behind him unsteadily, devoid of life, looking at no one, holding a huge, thick garland befitting the glory of a princess and equally disgraceful for the pledge it was destined to impose.

Like a stone, I progressed, passing from one seat to another. The kings rose, grimaced and left. And then I heard, 'Hastinapur.' Even in heart-broken grief, the name of the kingdom reminded me of the great Bhishma's vow. The sudden brief familiarity with the country made me stop. I realized what I had done when the gathering erupted in hearty cheer, assuming the halt to be my consent for the man standing beside me. When I didn't move, Vasudev gently lifted my hand to have the garland placed around him. The news spread faster than light. People of the kingdom waiting outside for an update, screamed, 'Long live, King Pandu. Long live Queen Kunti. God bless Hastinapur!' I looked up to face the man, who had just transformed me from a princess into a queen.

The king who stood before me looked pale and weak, bereft of energy, eyes drowsy and arms lethargic. There was a kind of rudderless withdrawal in the way he looked around, an eccentric lack of life-force. Standing quite close, I could also sense cruelty. For some time, I observed him, carefully evaluating his gestures. Elderly ladies teased that the bride was visibly head over heels for the groom, foretelling the companionship for seven auspicious births. The man in front blushed but wasn't excited, nor happy. He seemed to be there in acceptance of whatever life had in store for him; as if he wouldn't have felt any insult, had I walked past him like I did others in the queue. The partition of my hair bled with vermilion. From behind the holy music and shower of juvenile flowers, I heard destiny bursting into a wicked laughter. I had longed for Indra, the most handsome and powerful warrior. The one I was standing with, appearing like a coy bride, was such an offensive joke, a disaster in body and mind, both. Will this man father my children? Is this man even worthy of partnering with me in building the future of my dreams?

*

'Surya, is this your revenge? A curse that you never pronounced?' I looked up at the noon sky; the rays hurt, but I didn't bother.

A thin sheen of cloud came rushing to reduce the effect of his energy.

'No, Queen. Never.' I heard Surya's sigh. 'I try to stay away from Indra, though our paths cross in more ways than one. And you, I can never harm.'

'Why shouldn't you? You have every right and might.' I ignored Surya's connection with Indra. He still answered.

'Indra is not only a senior by hierarchy, but also a rival-friend! He has stood by me in the past, as he would in future. But our allies have been on warring terms. Indra's son Bali was defeated by my son Sugreeva with the aid of Vishnu's incarnation Rama many centuries ago.

The reverse is waiting to happen in the future. Such is the balance of the cosmos.'

Surya's voice was pensive, sadness from the reminiscence evident.

I didn't understand why Surya was telling me this aspect of history. 'And me?' I asked, hoping he would refuse to interfere between me and Indra. Instead, he stumped me again.

'You are the soul-companion of Surya. I cannot abandon you, till you abandon your academic prowess. I cannot destroy you either. My love for you grows with your attention to detail and isn't necessarily insulted by your loyalty towards another man. Because that loyalty, that commitment, is also a characteristic strength bestowed by Surya!'

6

That was the last night I was to have to myself. Accompanied by the crowd of cheerleaders, I crashed in the corner of the wall that separated me from the new groom. I had heard of kings making mischievous attempts to enter the rooms of the bride, only to be sent away by the friends of the newlywed girl amid squeals of laughter. No such delight was remotely awaited here. Women inside my chamber sang songs of fertility to charge up my body for the impending reception, while waiting for Pandu to make an advent. After midnight hours passed, they all yawned and fell asleep. I was left alone, fatigued and haunted by the deadly night.

The morning took me away from Kuntibhoja to the kingdom of Hastinapur, my new home. In an elaborate *palki*, I was dispatched with a few other women attendants and a count of soldiers, elephants, horses and gold as gifts. Pandu, my husband, rode a horse beside me. How strange it was that we were now expected to share a life together! I, Kunti, who wouldn't deign to look at those who didn't deserve to interrupt her eyesight, was now accompanying a strange, reclusive man as his demure wife. I was unsure of everything that was to unfold, devoid of any thrill and anticipation of a newlywed bride. After a long and exhaustive journey when we finally reached Hastinapur, I was welcomed by the queen, Gandhari, her eyes covered with a blindfold. It felt uncomfortable; a lot more than the eyes seemed hidden behind that piece of cloth. Vermilion was smeared on my forehead; flowers were showered on Pandu and me, amidst chants and cheers for Hastinapur. My husband stood reluctantly; his footsteps hesitant to lead me inside. When he faltered, I looked up and walked forward confidently with the husband trailing behind, filling an army of well-wishers with awe.

Gandhari smiled affectionately and held my hand.

'Uncle Bhishma, our Pandu is a married man now. Wouldn't you bless the couple?' she called out with great excitement. From behind Gandhari, I looked up at the man I had heard so much about, now my uncle-in-law. A warrior of might and valour, body as fit as it could be, eyes with the lustre of stars and zero signs of belonging to a generation before – Bhishma looked more an eligible bachelor than the man I was married to. What must have been his life in celibacy! He didn't look bothered, though. I bent to touch his feet with great respect and he blessed generously. I moved on to meet others in the family, still strangely fascinated by the uncle-in-law.

'See who has come to meet you.' The irony in Gandhari's exuberance made the blind prince cringe. The innocent, elegant man, who had uttered no protest, had been denied the crown, citing his disability. I walked past the graceful lady to hold his hands within my palms. He grew stiff but relaxed soon and blessed.

'Why have you brought her here on her first day at Hastinapur? Show her the gardens and the orchards; take her to the northern terrace where the birds sing songs of spring throughout the year.' He lifted a casket kept beside and held it forward.

'I wanted to meet my elder brother-in-law. Pandu had been telling me how he was often outwitted by his brother during childhood.' I lied under my breath while accepting his gift. Dhritarashtra smiled pleasantly and forgot about the singing birds.

'He did? That's true. I learnt the verses faster than Pandu and ...'

'Let her rest now.' Gandhari interrupted. 'We have our whole lives to chat in peace. Kunti must be tired after a long journey.' Dhritarashtra frowned but didn't object. He removed his hands from over my palm. I wanted to say that I wasn't tired but countering Gandhari didn't feel wise.

The air in the house made it clear that everything here was systematized by pre-defined protocols.

I had seen Dhritarashtra before, in my astrological vision. An entire machinery of the house worked towards suppressing his voice, disabling him from appreciating his toned arms! He had learnt to feel insecure by every little progress of Pandu. There was no resentment in the man but life must have bullied him too many times.

I moved on to a cabin introduced as mine. Food was served. Pandu was nowhere. Gandhari advised me to rest. Lying on my back and staring at the ceiling, I could hear the footsteps of Bhishma from afar, walking in haste and in authority. I smiled. Bhishma may have taken a binding vow, but nature conspired to make him the leader from behind the throne. Why else would the elder prince be blind and the crown prince shaken in his shoes? I didn't know when sleep overtook me.

*

Compared to the peaceful abode of my father, Hastinapur was constantly in a state of bustle. There was always a discussion brewing, something to acquire or recover, a rebel whom Bhishma would tame with great mastery – sometimes with love, else by intimidation. Few days into the palace and I had realized the jewelled country was devoid of a capable ruler. Bhishma, who was running it, refused to name himself the king. Dhritarashtra was constrained by his physical limitations. Pandu was not concerned, lacking even the usual life-zest, though he was upstaged with the crown. He was an adept warrior, riding towards rival kingdoms in speed, smashing any insurgence with ruthless might and returning to his reclusive corner as if he didn't exist. He left for an expedition soon after we were married. When I marked his forehead with the auspicious sandalwood and vermilion, while wishing him victory on his mission, I saw a strange cruelty in his eyes again. With the sword in hand, Pandu looked barbaric.

Those were not the characteristics of a leader. Pandu wasn't one, either by attitude or by interest. It seemed he didn't live for himself; he existed because he couldn't die! Bhishma controlled everything, from instructing Dhritarashtra to motivating Pandu from time to time, so the reality of his failures remained concealed from outsiders.

On one of those days, I was taking rounds through the mansion. I was trying to shake some of the windows that must have remained closed for centuries. One door led to the other, each wall echoing subtle displeasure at the audacity of a curious queen. I lost myself to the pride of stony corridors which had witnessed a dynasty of glorious kings with a legacy of courage, simultaneously setting benchmarks with their momentous slips and historical blunders. I touched those pillars trying to gauge the period of the architecture, unaware that I had entered such compounds which women didn't frequent. The guards in the quarters were taken aback, unsure of whether they should warn and request me to back off. They stepped forward to initiate action but were discouraged by the disdain in my body language that knew how to keep unwanted intruders off my path. I walked ahead, leaving them wide-eyed behind. The large door heavy with iron latches seemed alluring. With my usual zest, driven by an irresistible temptation to investigate what treasure deserved such strict conservation, I tried to unlatch and push it open. The chains didn't move by half a nail. Disappointed and angry, I stepped back, only to clash against a broad chest. Jolted, I turned around to find Bhishma looking down at my wide, shaken eyes, with affection and amusement. Without a word, he pulled the latch with enormous strength and set the chains free, banging loudly below. He pushed the door backwards. It opened with an ominous sound, menacing with the stability of the foundation. Bhishma walked inside and gestured me to follow.

This was a colossal hall housing the weapons of the kingdom. Neatly arranged on racks on the wall and on the ground, serviced regularly, scarily ready for use. Multiple flights of stairs in the corners lead to vestibules above and basements below, all of which were packed with countless destructibles, revered like lavish wealth – acquired, gifted and inherited. I looked around, wondering how many lives each of those would boast to have taken, stepping back unknowingly.

'I didn't know,' I tried to reason as Bhishma smiled down from his height.

'This is a good sign, my child. Good fortune for you and auspicious for the dynasty.' Royal diplomacy had its own ways to explain offence like a favour. 'If the uninformed footsteps of the newlywed queen has brought her to the great house of weapons, it is destiny's indication towards a lion-hearted warrior to grace this dynasty with his holy birth.'

I didn't know about destiny's indication, but Bhishma's manifesto was quite clear. What a resolute, remorseless politician! Or was he just being a typical elder expressing his longing for an heir?

Nevertheless, his words crashed on me like a curse. An heir meant having a child with Pandu!

Palms sweating suddenly, heart pounding like it would fall out of my chest, and the blood leaving my face, I fumbled for words. I forgot to blush at the uncle-in-law's ambitious blessing. Not that Bhishma missed the change, but to my relief, he interpreted it differently. With compassion, he led me outside as the guards struggled to lock the door again. 'I understand our intelligent, new queen has bigger interests than the confines of the women's chamber. I will fix it for you.' Before I knew what that meant, he looked towards his left and called out for someone. 'Vidur, why don't you act as a guide for Queen Kunti and take her through each nook and corner she intends to visit. Explain to her everything she desires to know about us.'

I dashed my head towards the direction from which a humble, 'Most certainly' had flown in. A thin, tall man with energy in his arms and intelligence in his eyes stood there. I wouldn't have known about his presence, had he not been addressed. I frowned with displeasure.

Bhishma blessed me and walked off in long strides. Watching him from behind, I wondered why he would leave me with this awkward man, who promised of a meritorious company but seemed to bear neither the Kshatriya lineage, nor the shine of a Brahman! Before disappearing from sight, Bhishma turned and I noticed a queer smirk on his face.

Suddenly it all dawned upon me!

Was he trying to pair me with another man because he suspected that Pandu's withdrawal may not fetch any grandchildren? Was this a conspiracy of the glorious, to spy upon the restless wife of an impotent man? My face flushed red. Anger frothing inside, I walked ahead on the brick steps, well aware that I was being followed, till I was back into the women's chambers where controversies didn't lead to scandals.

In this house, there were many!

7

The secrets flowing inside the women's chambers were bizarre. Windows were closed and the breeze was intermittent – it was hot and claustrophobic inside. Something or the other was always cooking, black smoke from the stoves suffocated the space before whirling outwards. Behind the smoke, subdued voices chuckled at the mention of Queen Satyavati who had, by then, retired into the forests. The daughter of the fisherman-king was clever enough to seduce King Shantanu and reduce the great Bhishma to a mere caretaker. How shrewd was her sense of politics that when her son Vichitravirya couldn't produce sons, she asked Rishi Vyasa to impregnate her daughters-in-law, Ambika and Ambalika. Disgusted with the petty gossip, I moved on into the interiors where limited attendants were permitted to enter, that too, only when summoned. Gandhari sat there in grace, daylight adding prominence to her sharp features. She smiled. 'Where have you been, Kunti? I don't see you often on these premises.'

I smiled back and held her hand. 'How will you see me when you have consciously chosen not to?' I said, unable to contain any longer that her blindfold had piqued my curiosity.

This time, she laughed out loud. 'When one of your senses is inactive, the rest of them come together to fill in the gap. Since I don't see, my ears can detect footsteps from a distance. And I can tell who it is by their smell.' She lowered her voice. 'Don't ever mistake it for a handicap. Such belief might land you in a disaster.' She laughed again.

Extreme strength emerges from immense pain. I remained quiet.

'What happened, Kunti? Why this silence?' Gandhari asked.

'I do not mean to think of you as feeble, Sister. You are a woman of great capabilities, of which I have the least doubts. I came to derive some of that.' I said, hoping to melt her heart, which must have become immune to agony by now. Not that the lady was to be swayed by my diplomacy so easily. She caught me off guard by asking something totally out of context.

'Why did you come to me seeking an explanation for this self-blinded face, Kunti? Women in the chambers gossip about it all day. Aren't you satisfied with their inputs, rich with monstrous sarcasm? They'd confer all so generously, without even being asked. What brings you to me?'

This time, it was my turn to smile. 'That would have been a truly overflowing resource to explore. But I'm afraid it would gloss every information with insipid mendacity. The unlawful hearsay would provide all, barring just what would promptly service my curiosity with to-the-point information!'

We both burst into laughter.

Gandhari stretched her hand and held mine, drawing me closer. I sat next to her. The huge wooden swing moved to and fro, as its owner gathered herself to disclose a morsel from her heart, perhaps for the first time since she lay her feet on this establishment. She didn't make any effort to tell me the reason why she had blindfolded herself. It was available in the air, sometimes respectfully, otherwise as impolite gibberish served with absurd rumours. She told me the consequences, instead.

'This house doesn't understand love, Kunti, neither does it value personal commitments. Or relationships. If I may put it very bluntly, no one belongs to anyone here. Everyone has sworn fealty to the family. Decisions are sovereign, not democratic, and strictly political. Nothing is exclusive here, not even with your parents, nor your children. In the palace of vast inheritance and endowments, nothing or no one is truly yours.'

None of this was shocking. Bhishma's affection had felt fake. There was a shrewdly crafted distance between individuals, which I had no intention to correct. People were cordial but cold.

'Stay prepared to be used or exploited as per the needs of the dynasty.' Gandhari pronounced. My jaw tightened. She placed the palm of her left hand on my right. 'How will you adapt if its mere mention accelerates your breath?'

She smiled, but her empathy shook from its confidence when I asked, 'Could you be a little more direct about what you have been instructed to tell me?'

Gandhari took some deep breaths before she opened her mouth again. 'You are intelligent. I don't think I'd be required to say much. You are part of the system already. Swim carefully unless you wish to be whirled downwards.'

Feeling a sudden bad taste in my mouth, I got up to leave. Gandhari didn't stop me, having guessed my revulsion. Just before I walked out, she mentioned, 'Sisters-in-law do not always make for trusted relationships. But I am willing to be a friend, in case you need one. I wasn't offered such an award when I was greeted at the entrance with vermilion and blessings.'

'I will come back,' I assured and put my steps forward.

*

'How is he, Surya?'

I asked one of those days, while watching Pandu practise sword-fighting with one of his generals, my fingers clutched upon a limpid red ruby dangling at the tip of my neck. It was Surya's parting gift to me. I held it like it was more precious than my life. On the translucent surface of the stone, I could see myself in a way no one ever could. My flaws and my shortcomings were mirrored, as were my youth and intelligence.

With a sudden stroke, the general lost his grip. A large object came flying towards the door and ripped apart the silk curtain, exposing my hidden seat. I lifted a hand to catch the wild beast by the tail just before it could strike and threw it on the white floor with a grimace. It trembled at the humiliation before going still. Instead of nurturing the soldier who may have hurt himself, Pandu bent forward to pick the fallen sword. His eyes met mine. They weren't perplexed with the knowledge of my presence; neither did mine make any attempt to withdraw. I was looking at him, though lost in another world. Quietly, he retreated to the space of his comfort. I was restless.

'He is fine, in good company, growing up well and bathing every day in my rays,' Surya confirmed.

'Is he being mothered well?' I was not sure whether I would have been happy to hear that he wasn't. That he needed me. That he longed for the mother who birthed him, over the mother who adopted him. Karn, my son with Surya! A secret kept away from the universe, a life growing apart from me with each passing moment, since the time I had trusted the newborn into his father's care. A child I had no chances of owning again, or seeing anytime soon. But Surya would never lie. He didn't even know how to present a difficult truth with polite diplomacy.

'He is being mothered so well; he considers his foster mother to be his birthing mother, unless anyone mentions it. Angrily then, he tries to correct the intruder, explaining that he was Radha's son, born to someone else by mistake and duly returned. He is a strong boy – brave, disciplined and active.'

Surya's light suddenly felt too merciless. Father Kuntibhoja's words that had filled my heart once, had been passed on to my son, only to be used for another lady! I was no more than a 'someone else'. I didn't even have the luxury of blaming anyone for my misfortune. It was my folly. It was my own choice! The consequences that would follow, would also be for me to suffer alone. I didn't yet know what it was, but had mentally prepared myself for the worst punishment a woman could be subjected to.

Some decisions are tough and political. After a childhood full of dreams and an adolescence full of ambition, when I was about to explore and achieve, the child was forced upon me as a trophy I wasn't ready for. The beautiful, innocent face of

Karn felt like that opponent of war who I could neither fight, nor defeat.

My insides calmed at the thought of Bhishma. Didn't I understand his politics, having come from the same corridors? But I promised myself to be careful around this man and his moves. In my world, my politics wouldn't be overshadowed by that of others.

I observed Pandu from a distance, whenever I could. There was no arousal of love or lust, but it did tell me a little about him. I saw him practising wrestling and archery, not with great wit but with sufficient expertise of a king who had been thoroughly coached by his well-wishers. His credentials failed when Bhishma was nearby. Those weaker than him, he attacked like a blood-thirsty tiger. Typical signs of a weak personality. Not that he wasn't interested in a woman's body, but he lacked the courage to gather himself for any conversation or action. He was the kind to wait for things to happen.

The arrangement worked well for me. I wasn't interested in Pandu amorously in the least. I remembered Durvasa's words, 'I advise you to detach when the world seems unworthy of your brilliance, only to preserve the finesse that you have built within yourself with such care.'

The sage must have tried to prepare me for the loveless marriage I was destined for. But Gandhari's incomplete warning kept looming over me. 'Stay prepared to be used or exploited as per the needs of the dynasty.'

What did it mean? Something was definitely roasting in the royal pots and I needed to get to the bottom of it. I didn't want to be taken by shock while being pushed into the labyrinth of a dark well, disguised by a cover of lotus petals. I walked back into the women's chambers, feigning some work that kept me acutely occupied. The ladies were surprised at my arrogance, having entered their territories without knocking formally and reshuffling things on their shelves. The buzz resumed shortly after, though. All kinds of conversations, concoctions, capsuled into banters – half truth and half judgment. I passed through them all, eyes targeted afar but ears alert to pick the right clue. I stopped abruptly towards the western gate.

'Vyasa was intimidating and scary,' I heard. 'When queen Ambika saw him, she was so terrified, her eyes shut automatically. The child born to her was the blind Dhritarashtra.'

'When Vyasa foretold the future to Satyavati, she was taken aback. Unwilling to yield, she sent for Ambalika.' Another voice floated in. 'Poor thing turned pale looking at him, but knew better than closing her eyes, having been pre-warned by Satyavati. Her child, Pandu, was born weak and under-confident, no visible disability but mentally rejecting all.'

I stood there, unable to move, my ears piqued at the very next statement. 'And then there was a third child!' Giggles followed. 'When both attempts failed at producing a deserving heir to the dynasty, Satyavati ordered Ambika to go in again. This time Ambika sent a maid to fill in for her. The lowly caste was neither scared, nor disappointed. No loathing, neither resentment, true to her identity of a loyalist to the royalty, she performed her task with great finesse and birthed Vidur, half-Brahmin by birth and a Kshatriya by upbringing.'

With a dagger shoved down my throat, I turned and proceeded towards the exit, to process the information I had just been privy to. My feet slowed down again, when elderly whispers along the way suggested something critical. 'Pandu is enormously hungry for beauty. He just doesn't know how to express.' A slandering voice chirped in. 'He was the result of a union where the appearance of the father dismayed the mother, remember? He was born with the suppressed sigh of his mother. The woman longed to be held with passion by the gorgeous, to be made love to by mutual attraction, not the needs of a dynasty. Pandu is desperate to feel that affection but is made impotent by his incapacity to ask for it.'

This was received with offensive laughter. 'The poor thing is trapped under the shadow of his mother. He needs to experience women who have lived life better than Ambalika. The day he meets such a beauty, he will find his stability. He will then talk for himself instead of being coddled by others!'

Having had enough for the day, I ran back into my room and buried my head into a pillow. A vast amount of information formed into thoughts, raising the most strenuous questions and resettling them with complicated answers. It was a sleepless night. In the wee hours of the morning, I went back to my dashboard, untangling complicated calculations to reach the planetary positions of a preferred date from a few decades ago. But even the greatest mastery of astrology could only offer glimpses, never the whole. Not even with the generous blessings of Surya, who observed all three facades of time with simultaneous attention.

8

That morning, I ventured out to the great palace garden, walking unmindfully on the sun-kissed, freshly rained-upon grass, a hundred thoughts crossing my mind. The branches criss-crossing from above played with the light and shadows. Bullocks swayed in herds of six or seven, walking into the blue waters of the pool laced with innumerable lotus leaves, a few of which had started budding. Fallen petals from the tiny mogra and large magnolia mingled with the water like eternal consorts. The vast pool indeed was the flirtatious king to many queens, engaged in their leisurely pastime of chasing birds with ripples. Little beings quacked and rose upwards, flapping their wings in protest, only to fall back again and sail through. Mild breeze rustled through the leaves, smiling and cautioning. God knows for how long I sat there, witnessing the magnificence of nature, when something felt unusual. I whirled around and was startled to find Vidur standing a few steps away, supporting himself against an ashoka tree, watching me in silence.

'What are you doing here?' I said sharply, my voice dipped in displeasure.

Vidur didn't he move an inch from the corner. 'The friend you are looking for in your loneliness, is me, Queen. I know what is happening with you. I can help.' Somehow the calm in his voice was far more threatening than my impudence.

'I don't need any help, unless the royal servants are appointed to spy on the women of the house,' I spat back with anger at the audacity of this man, offering his friendship to me, Kunti, who ranked much higher in status. But Vidur was made up of a different network of nerves, unlikely to lose connection.

'What if the royal servant can take you to such a truth that the women's chamber can't; Gandhari wouldn't and Bhishma, you would never ask?' He said with a spark in his eyes and a hidden smile on the lips which irritated me further. He sat down towards the corner of the ashoka tree, making no attempts to level himself with my stature in the family. He seemed rather keen to accept my rebuke and maintain the distance that a queen must have with an attendant, in sarcastic response to my prejudice. I wasn't one to melt so easily either, but something about this man told me he held the answers to many of my questions about my new family. The illustrious dynasty of warriors preened from a distance. Inside the close-knit borders of the palace, one of the stakeholders was blind and the other didn't know how to use his vision. The rest were happily mute. He seemed the sole person willing to invite me into the secrets.

But why? I was sceptical and clenched my jaw.

'Queen, you have come with your own blessings and curses, the rewards of which will be enjoyed by this family. But they will also have to embrace the sufferings that you bring along. Your fears are baseless. No one in his house will be able to establish any domination over you, howsoever big he might be, because anyone that opposes you will have to first fight the sun god!'

Caught off guard, I turned at this imposture. 'What do you mean?' I asked, my voice trembling.

Vidur didn't answer my question. 'You may think I am Bhishma's right-hand man and an obsequious moron. But I am also blessed by Yama, the Dharmaraj, the guiding force to man's journey on earth, if one cares to listen to that voice!' He paused, without removing his gaze. 'You are the knowledgeable and calculative Kunti, Queen. You can work out for yourself what is right for Pandu. I will ensure there are no interferences from any corner.'

He got up to leave and turned again. 'You are safe here, Queen. As safe as your son is now, many miles away, under the Surya's watchful eyes! They call him *Suta-putra*. Don't you feel burdened about his well being. Just love him. Bless him.'

A cold shiver ran down my spine. How did he know! By then, Vidur had disappeared amidst the many shades of the garden. I was too dumbstruck to stop him and ask. With the brief mention of Suta-putra, meaning son of the Suta caste – that is neither Brahmin nor Kshatriya – Vidur had just thrown a sword ahead, lancing through my arrogance towards those I considered unworthy, with pompous, self-manicured superiority. Was my son being humiliated as a Suta-putra, his talents deemed inferior because of a birth-history which wasn't under his capacity to revise?

I crashed back on the grass, memories turning me blue.

*

That day I had given myself to Surya, so both of us could be freed from the cast of the spell, it wasn't a union of love, but more of obligation. Surya promised to keep me guarded from my immediate interests. Making love with Surya implied that my virginity would be restored, fertility enhanced, body refined and intelligence exfoliated. When I returned to my palace at Kuntibhoja's kingdom, everything was moving at its usual pace and no one had woken up to my brief disappearance. The god was controlling the hours of daylight. The union with Surya had introduced me to the wonders of the body. It had only enhanced my longing for Indra. While my mind kept searching for the lord of my dreams, I registered certain changes in my body. New life was growing inside me. Surya had assured that the consequence of our union wouldn't be witnessed by anyone else but only the two of us. The growing bulge in the middle of my body was hidden from others. It was only for me to attend to the bubble before my belly, where life had started kicking with the energy of a beginner. It felt uncomfortable but it was also the most divine touch to be felt on earth. How unfortunate are fathers to be deprived of this heavenly encroachment!

On the night of labour, Surya appeared beside

me. With a soothing smile, he held my hand. The pain didn't subside but the consciousness of birthing another human took precedence over self-distress. A healthy and hearty Karn arrived with shrill cries – his authority evident from his vigour. Surya lovingly armoured him with the *kavach kundala,* which would protect him from every danger. He lifted the child in his arms and watched his face. 'He will be a great hero by his own might, Kunti. The kavach kundala would do nothing more than passing a fatherly affection.' Though said with pride, that every father has upon holding his son, I felt the deep, lamenting sigh of Surya filling up the room.

'What happened, Deva?' I asked.

Surya mentioned with resolute seriousness, 'This child will grow up to be a selfless giver. As giving as his father and as ambitious as his mother. He will be a brave warrior for the world to remember. He wouldn't need the protection of these armours, ever. Only once when circumstances fail him, will he need their strength. But that is just when someone would seek it from him and he would be generous enough to give it away, knowing well that the benevolence would cost him his life!'

'Who? Who would take it away from him?' I asked, exasperated.

'Could be you. Or someone very dear to you,' Surya said grimly.

A new mother, that too, at a very tender age, battling with the realization that I would have to part with the child by morning, I wasn't in a state of mind to comprehend Surya's loathsome riddles. Why would I, a mother, take away the armour that would protect my son from evils? Irritated, I set aside the absurdity of that suggestion. Hadn't we decided that Karn would stay under the watchful eyes of his father? Hadn't Surya promised that I would be updated about his whereabouts from time to time? The deva was testing my nerves.

Surya didn't continue further. I held the baby boy close to my body. He seemed to love my warmth as much as I adored his softness. I had only one night with this child, concealed from the rest of the world. I kissed the child a thousand times and fed him the nectar of my body, which was meant to protect him from internal harms. I changed his clothes a number of times, played with his little fingers and feet, laughing at the antics and shedding tears at the impending separation. That one night was all I had to live a lifetime of motherhood with Karn.

The bright morning seemed darker than the trapping inside an iron mine. Surya assured me the child would grow well under his invigilation. He mentioned kindly that nothing would ever be kept from me, until the child took charge of his life. I filled a large basket with food and money, covered the baby with warm clothes and held him close to my chest. Little hands circled around my neck, secured by the mother's love engulfing him. Little did the newborn know that this privilege wasn't meant to last. As he blissfully slept, I put the child in the basket and let it flow on the Ganga, bidding a tearful farewell to my first born. As the wind and the water took him away from me, voices inside accused me of cruelty and warned of this day's consequences.

I came to know later, Karn had been adopted by a charioteer named Adhiratha and was now popularly known as Adhiratha-putra! Or Radheya, by the name of his mother.

How on earth did Vidur know this? The sun god had promised our secret would never be disclosed to anyone. I looked accusingly at the glowing fireball in the sky.

'Deva, did you not keep your word? You spoke to others about Karn?'

'No, Kunti.' Mild rays fell on me through the branches. 'Vidur is indeed blessed by Yama, my son with Saranyu. Information, like blessings, pass from one brain to another by lieu of inheritance! He knows everything. And he knows when not to reveal secrets. You can trust him, Queen. He will be your greatest ally in times of distress. Don't you think of him as an uneducated servant. If anyone deserves your friendship on earth, it is he.'

I looked aside sceptically, my mind racing through the series of events I had witnessed in Hastinapur. Surya's voice floated in again, whispering into my ear.

'You can discuss with Vidur that part of your heart, which you keep away of everyone else in the world. He will steer you out from all sadness, every harm. He is a friend who will offer protective advice to you and your family, when danger will lurk at your door without your knowledge. You will be forewarned against plots of murder, you will be assisted to adopt diplomatic means calmly on the face of troubles.'

I remembered those visuals I had in Surya's chamber, of a castle burning and a man helping five young men and a woman to escape. I remembered now, I had seen there none other than Vidur. But who were those running out from the burning house? Me and my children? My children with Pandu?

Surya interrupted again, restricting my thoughts going haywire. 'Driven by the fairness of the Dharmaraj, Vidur will stand up for you when no one else can. And he will also steer Bhishma's politics so it doesn't clash with your priorities.'

Somewhat pacified, I tried to concentrate on everything I had learned in the last few days. Pandu could be brought back to strength in the company of feminine intervention. That femininity was not mine. I would have to act on it before Bhishma devised ways to get his heir through other means.

Not that I didn't have it in mind already.

A few days back we had been to the kingdom of Madra, to attend a royal function. I had to accompany Pandu as a formality. King Shalya of Madra was at his hospitable best. They spoke about their alliance with Hastinapur and sealed the exchange treaty for cattle, horses and medicinal herbs. In their internal chambers, the women were voluptuous, full-lipped, with long hair and gleaming skin. It was difficult to look away from them, having cast a glance. Unlike in Hastinapur, the people of Madra were born artists – their words flew like poetry, voice melodious, dipped in appreciation and gratitude for each other. I was being attended by Princess Madri, the sister of King Shalya. In contrast to my reserve, she was like the rippling waves of a vivacious river, laughing unbarred, well aware but not chained by her beauty. But more than that, what made Madri irresistibly attractive was her inherent happiness. She was a naturally happy woman, with or without all her possessions, capable of sucking anyone into her state of mind!

I had seen Madri and Pandu exchanging glances. I would be surprised if they hadn't. Madri was just the potion that Pandu was thirsty for. He needed one person to prove before him that life could indeed be beautiful and people were worth loving; Madri was a living example of every stimulant, wide awake to the effect of her presence on a man's desires. But neither had crossed their lines. Madri was intelligent enough to restrain when I was a consular guest aiding her kingdom's infrastructural growth. And Pandu didn't have the confidence to go ahead and initiate.

Once back in Hastinapur, I called for Vidur inside my private chamber, shocking the palace and its naysayers. There were storms inside the women's chamber, the young queen having invited another man into her private abode. I answered none; Vidur entered fearlessly. I told him to get Pandu married to Madri, as that would strengthen the king with attributes that only Madri can bring.

Vidur smiled through it. 'And this wedding would also set you free from some of the obligations.'

Pointless to hide anything further, I smiled back.

Pandu and Madri were married in a quiet ceremony, a few days after.

9

True to the prophesying voices of the women's chamber, Pandu showed visible changes soon after he was hitched. His new wife wasn't the one to stay within the codes of royal etiquettes. From my window, I saw her pulling Pandu out into the orchard and vanishing into the trees. Late in the nights, I would hear them talking on the terrace, hand in hand, soaking in the moonlight. When the women of the family got together to bathe in the huge centrally located pool, she would sprinkle water at others and laugh like a spring, getting all to follow suit. She smiled at everyone, irrespective of their social status. The palace was injected with new life by her mere presence. Everyone asked for Madri whenever she wasn't around. Her ingrained exuberance touched everyone, including Pandu. He seemed to have suddenly woken up from a slumber. In his morning exercises, I could sense a vigour. Pandu reached the court before time, checked the samples of new weapons himself before discussing their procurement with Bhishma, went for rounds through the city, summoned the traitors to warn or punish. While crossing his corridors, I found him bent over a large map with peasants on one side and engineers on the other, inspecting the designs of proposed underground waterpipes for faraway, rain-starved farmlands. I smiled and carried on.

Even Bhishma was happy with the sudden developments, though it had taken Vidur quite some cajoling to convince him for Pandu's second marriage. He stopped me in the palace veranda soon after, to offer his congratulations.

'I always had a hunch, Queen, that you have the ability of foreseeing the future. You aren't a simple individual born just to make a man happy; you are the one to guide him forth to success.' He paused. 'Life never ceases to prove my learning wrong and force me to relearn. Seldom have I seen a woman so secure in her space that she can share her rights so effortlessly. Such are the qualities of a king, Kunti, not just a queen!'

As much as Bhishma was happy with Madri's intervention in improving Pandu's personality, he never allowed her to assume a position of power. I was to stand beside Pandu in all formal ceremonies. Madri stood with the other women in an area reserved for watching but not participation. Bhishma often sent for me to discuss various issues related to the country or the family, seeking my opinion.

'Kunti, we're planning to establish touch points at the grassroots. There would be regular gatherings, activities and exchanges. Would you like to work out a plan?' He offered and was pleasantly surprised when I went back with edutainment options to break the ice between the subjects and the royalty, make all laugh together through fun games and still exchange valuable life lessons. He invited me to the house of weapons when new ammunitions were procured and watched keenly as I looked on, neither with disdain, nor with enthusiasm.

'Consider sending the frontline soldiers to address the touch points at the grassroots.' I advised. 'Let them make merry with the people. As much as our soldiers need rugged training for warfare, we should also create circumstances for them to love the life brewing inside their country.'

Bhishma caught me wandering aimlessly, looking afar at nothing, engaged me in issues of finance and economics, and left happily with my suggestions.

Though my married life had been taken care of, Bhishma never allowed me to detach!

It was on one of these days that Pandu declared he wanted to go for hunting, shocking the house and its inhabitants. The young king wasn't known to be appreciative of these finer whims. No one knew when he had suddenly picked up on interests that he was so resistant to, till some time back. Accompanied by a few friends and attendants, holding his bow and a quiver of arrows with confidence, Madri winking at him with mischievous smiles, Pandu left for the forests, only to return to Hastinapur, a few days after having committed a blunder.

Some people are truly cursed. Indulgence isn't for them to relish; happiness isn't meant to last. Alas!

That autumn, the chorus of the crickets advanced into a late-night rendition as shadowy apparitions cheered through gusty winds. Pandu returned all alone in the dark, without informing anyone about his homecoming. Not a single soul was waiting to welcome him at the entrance. He dodged all rituals and went straight into his private chamber, locking himself there, barring all from paying a visit. His conviction was at an all-time low, perhaps shallower now than he had been before meeting Madri. In fact, he avoided Madri as if she was a demon. Bhishma met me with great urgency on one of those days, requesting my intervention. I promised I'd think about it but couldn't really comprehend how I could help when neither his confidence, nor the lack of it, was my doing. But I couldn't delay my visit when Madri came rushing into my chambers and fell before me, weeping. I hugged her as tightly as I could, feeling her restless nerves on my chest. Her tears washed my shoulders. Vermilion revolting in the parting of her hair, her pretty face was suddenly barren. Only the heartless could stay immune to such pleas. I looked at her with empathy. This girl didn't have anything else in her life other than her countenance and Pandu. Post their wedding, she hadn't been attributed the position of the prime queen, though she possessed the heart of the reigning king. She never complained, content with what had been offered to her. She had pulled Pandu out of his own pit, single-handedly. What evil could have come between the two today?

The same evening, I walked through the huge door behind which Pandu had locked himself. Burdened with the king's dictat to not allow anyone inside, the guards came to stop me, but couldn't muster the courage to utter the words. I walked forward uninterrupted and pushed the elaborate wooden door open. Inside, I heard the whimpering sound of a man in suffering. Boldly, I stepped forward.

In the last few months, Pandu's physique had improved. His arms were tighter now, chest pumping better breath, skin shining. The aura he had acquired hadn't completely vanished, but he seemed scared.

'What's troubling you?' I asked as calmly as I could. Pandu looked up, exasperated.

'Sit, Kunti,' was his first invitation to me to do anything in his presence.

For a while, we sat facing each other, I, unsure of how I was expected to help and Pandu, unwilling to speak. I watched him fiddling restlessly, at times, else stranded like a stone, trapped in some internal darkness.

Pandu was longing for a neutral presence – not a wife, nor a lover, neither a well-wisher, not even God! Sometimes the best companionship is to spend time together, though not necessarily with each other. It allows you to have your space without feeling lonely. With great patience, I waited till I found him covering his face with his hands. 'I have landed into a deep mess, Queen.'

*

'How could you do that!' I asked, my insides cringing.

'I didn't see them, Kunti. I just heard the groans of a deer. I didn't know what they were doing. I was only aware of their presence.' He tried to reason.

'This is sin.' I lamented.

'That's what I am told and hence, I am cursed.' He agreed.

For some time, my head was spinning. How would we manage to turn around this situation?

Deep inside the forest, Pandu had followed a sound and shot a few arrows, expecting to have fallen a deer. When the traumatic gasps of human suffering surfaced, he rushed in that direction and found Rishi Kindama in deep pain as his wife lay dead beside him. Lustfully attracted to each other, the couple was making love in the position of deer, amusing each other in pretence of the wonderful creatures, moaning like the animals in great delight, when Pandu's arrows had caused the fatal interruption.

'What kind of brute raises arms on a mating couple, you savage predator!' The rishi had lamented in great pain, shouting hoarse. Before Pandu could clarify, he uttered a terrible curse. 'You wouldn't be spared of this offence so easily. If you ever try to make love with another woman, you will die, too!'

Pandu had dropped himself by now, grovelling to the sage for forgiveness and to take back the curse, claiming ignorance. But the man had succumbed to his injuries. Devastated, Pandu returned to the kingdom, unable to face anyone and explain the turn of events. Definitely not to the beautiful Madri.

I truly felt sad for him. Yet, there was nothing I could do to undo whatever had gone wrong. All I could try was to pull Pandu out of the abyss of self-pity and face the consequences. The curse was not going to restrict his personal life; its consequences would be far long-lasting. But this wasn't the night to mourn. That could wait. This was the time to strategize.

'What will I do with this life? What will I tell uncle Bhishma, who expects my progeny to take over the throne? How will I face Madri, whose love for me knows no bounds? Do I tell them that I was infertile before, now impotent, too!?' His voice was rising above the permissible levels that could keep things under wraps. 'I wanted to give up my life than come back here. But I am told that a childless man can't enter heaven. He must rot in hell.' Pandu wailed.

Though I never was emotionally invested in this man, witnessing him baring his guards felt hopeless. Now, at this befallen hour, Pandu was ready to let go of anything that stuck to him in the muddle called life.

'Whoever said that, didn't mean you can't reach heaven if you die childless.' I tried to explain. 'It meant that in each life, you must leave behind a legacy ...'

Pandu was too restless to understand the philosophy. He refused to listen. All he wanted was a quick recovery. 'Help me get out of this curse, Kunti.' He pleaded. I saw in his eyes the bottled-up tears of humiliation that a man is too ashamed to acknowledge.

It was not just a lame request to be set free from an unfair curse. Pandu was seeking from me way more than a man could ask of his wife. He wanted me to be his anchor. It was his most desperate endeavour to kick away a paralysis. Mortals are told that complete surrender happens in love. Yet, there is another surrender that happens through confession.

Pandu was trapped within a thick, tall wall pressing upon him from all sides. It was related to his mother!

Pandu was imploring that I demolish that invisible wall.

10

I lay below a giant tree, deep inside the forest. Thin insects gathered on its wall, walking upwards, oblivious that the colossal trunk would only offer them a mesh of branches to choose from and not every branch would lead to a ripe fruit oozing juice! Fungus and weeds spread themselves wherever they could; the rest of the earth was dusted by dry leaves. The sky was sparsely visible here, the top of it covered by a canopy of leaves. Sunlight permeated through the gaps above. Otherwise, it was dark around, not gloomy but mysterious. A fruit dropping suddenly startled us, our indiscretion made silly snakes raise their hoods before returning to their errands. From where I lay, I spotted the cuckoo stealthily laying its eggs in the nest of another bird. The golden voice is known for being nasty! Seeks pleasure but is unwilling to take responsibility. The world forgives the dubious act, swayed by its melodious talent. Such is the living world. When you are attractive, the filth is forgiven.

This forest didn't have the luxuries of the palace. But there was peace and adventure. There was little to carry, almost nothing to look back to. No protocols, no expectations, no obligations. The path ahead was unknown. We walked as far as we could, rested when we couldn't. We survived on the fruits we gathered on the way. One night, when the sounds of wild animals tore through our sanity, Madri covered her ears out of fright. I got up and looked for them, trying to figure their direction and calculate if we were in danger. Through the desolate and dark path, I trudged further, hearing nothing other than my own footsteps. Twelve elephants on the right, six boars in the north. They'd take less than two hours to reach us, I figured. The sky was overcast, but no other sign of rain. The weather was dry and tropical winds raised a storm. Madri and Pandu were fast asleep. By now, I had the complete map of the place inscribed in my head, I measured my steps to avoid the pits. Bawls of the elephants and boars were more anxious than intimidating. I may have walked away for quite some distance, obsessed and intrigued by the call of the wild, when a blast of fire shot skywards, a few miles ahead and spread into an entrancing round, trapping us all within its circumference. Stunned, I turned to look behind. Pandu lowered his arms, having released the rope of the bow, kindling the protective blaze around us. For the first time, I was mightily impressed. Till then, I had only heard about Pandu's proficiency with arms. Witnessing it thus, the word slipped my tongue much audibly. 'Incredible!'

Pandu had already started walking back. He turned to acknowledge the compliment. 'It is not unusual for warriors to be of use during life-threatening situations, but even more incredible is your fearlessness. What do you think were you up to?'

Only if I knew what I was up to! Curiosity had rushed me into umpteen troubles more than once. But old habits die hard.

Pandu nodded his head, knowing that I didn't have an answer and was reluctant to admit to my stupidity. He walked forward again and I followed with a sheepish smile.

Strangely, the forests revealed a different side of Pandu. He was far more relaxed, though Kindama's curse frustrated him to death. By the time we were back to our spot in the forest, he glanced at the sleeping face of Madri and looked at me.

'What is our plan from here, Kunti?'

Late in the night, it was an opportunity for us to speak in privacy.

'You have only left behind your palace, King. You will have to forego the baggage that comes with it.' I responded.

'Why did you call me "king"? Is that sarcasm?' Pandu asked fiercely, quite unlike the usual laidback man I had known. Getting him out of Hastinapur had started working already, without him knowing it. I smiled at the transformation. On the face of it, I countered him. 'Sarcasm lies not much in my calling you a king than you believing that you aren't!'

Outwitted, he tried to look away, smiling but not cheerful. His eyes landed on the sleeping Madri again, separated from him by a few forbidden steps. He watched her with lustful eyes, but didn't move from his position. Realizing he was being watched, he forced himself to turn.

'How have you forgiven me so easily, Kunti?' he asked and closed his eyes, sighing deeply.

My long-drawn sigh blended effortlessly with the gloom of the evening. 'I never had anything to take from you, King. Neither did you have anything to give. Had we tried, we would have forced ourselves on each other, perhaps to satisfy some social mores. But personally, we both would be unhappy being pulled into an act of disgrace.' I tried to explain and brought myself closer. 'Isn't it similar to what you are trying to run from?'

The question slapped him hard.

*

Convincing Bhishma that Pandu wanted to exile himself indefinitely with his wives was difficult. Vidur came forward in broad steps, to consult with me on whatever was happening. But I refused to divulge the reasons behind our decision. Pandu had depended on me for everything that happened hereafter. I explained to the patriarchy that this self-imposed exile would pull Pandu out of a temporary spell that the earlier excursion had cast on him. We will come back when Pandu would take over the throne, not because there was no better option, but because he deserved to do so. And we would come back with Pandu's children. No one stopped us anymore. Only Dhritarashtra kept showering gauche criticisms, admonishing Pandu for falling shamelessly within the diversions of the female. His voice lashed upon the concrete wall and was heard by all but attended by none.

When we set off for the long journey, Bhishma blessed us all but looked at me sharply to indicate that this would be regarded completely as my discernment. Success would be enjoyed by the house, but failure would inspect every aspect as my sedition. I looked away, lest I lashed back that this very man was to be blamed for Pandu's disastrous lifelessness! Those in the women's chamber still gossiped about his birth, mocking his mother for turning pale at the sight of Vyasa. Grandmother Satyavati is said to have approached her stepson Bhishma, to break his vow of celibacy and birth a Kshatriya prince for the throne. When the Kuru clan was in desperate need of an heir, Bhishma had shied away from committing the sin of breaking a vow, lest people called it his opportunism! Every human guards and grows his treasury but expects others to be selfless. The only option left was Satyavati's other son, Vyasa, the blood that comes from the extended family, infused with Brahmanical energy. Mother Ambalika didn't take to this union well. Pandu was conceived under a state of acute disgust, terror and repulsion – something the mother could never forget, nor could Pandu ever forego.

Brought up with withdrawal in his character and infertility in his mind, Pandu turned his back on everything new, especially when it came to sex. The mother couldn't ever put behind the memories of the night of horror, which severely affected his upbringing. The child's mind groped around with confusion and self-doubts brewing inside his system, wondering why he wasn't mothered like others, though he wasn't an orphan. Bhishma's strict invigilation had turned him into an expert warrior but left him to fight his inner battles alone. Adding generously to this complex situation were the hushed exchanges inside the women's quarters, where the child neglected by his mother may have run for shelter, only to be insulted and forced to continue with the guilt of his unwarranted birth. Pandu kept running from himself, feeling incomplete and trying to avenge on the battlefield, everything that defeated him inside a lonely room.

He grew up to be a catastrophic warrior, destroying his opponents ruthlessly, bringing back enormous wealth, expanding territories. But grossly inhumane! He attacked the rival nations, one after the other, as if his were the hands of Ambalika, holding the merciless sword to rip apart Vyasa – perhaps Satyavati, too. Bhishma couldn't be happier, Vidur never questioned. Pandu returned victorious, each time, as the man of the battlefield, his inner conflicts rested for the time being, appraising him rather than mocking at his masculinity.

Things started changing after he met Madri. With her beauty, innocence and unreserved acceptance, she had managed to tame Pandu's inner beast, treating him with unconditional love that didn't care for laurels. A face that stole glances and disappeared behind curtains distracted Pandu, while sealing a political treaty with her brother, Shalya. The spark in her eyes was irresistible, her touch as playful as a lover's and as caring as a mother's. Pandu held on to Madri like his lifeline, secretly acquiring self-esteem from her attention, his body warming up to hers.

Just when things were moving along perfectly, Kandima's curse had erected a wall that no sword could rupture, no arrow could destroy!

*

Startled, Pandu sat up on the grass. He looked at me with murderous eyes. Within a few moments, though, he fell back resigned as my resolve told him he could hide nothing, as I had observed far more than what he had meant to disclose.

'Is there anything I can do for you, Kunti? And for myself, too?' he asked, this time secure that his internal mess was being understood, not ridiculed. Not left unattended, but for the first time, addressed.

'For everything that goes away all so unfairly, there is always something unpredictable that you receive. Such is the rule of nature. It won't alter for you, either.' I asserted, leaving Pandu swimming among a host of questions, and turned, closing my eyes. He came flying towards me, turning me back towards him, demanding answers. My laughter echoed through the forest, as did his sigh.

'King, I was blessed by Rishi Durvasa to chant the mantras that can invoke gods and chain them to me, till I birth their child. You will not die childless.'

Pandu pushed backwards at such a blasphemous confession. His eyes bulged out of their sockets, unable to fathom the courage of a woman that pronounced such a difficult proposition so easily. How different would that be from his own birth story? Was history to repeat itself? Not till his arms had strength! His jaws tightened and fell, the vein on his forehead shot up, pushing the skin, principally abhorring the idea, yet conforming to the fact that he perhaps had very few alternatives left. That night, he couldn't sleep. I stayed awake with him, pretending to close my eyes in a deep slumber, so his privacy wasn't violated. He kept twisting and turning with great discomfort, hopelessly attempting to shield himself from the unacceptable proposal. All through the next day, he remained self-absorbed, smiling at Madri, performing all chores, but grossly unmindful. After two nights, when only the herd of deer rustled afar, he came back to finish the incomplete conversation. I had rehearsed the answer to his question several times in my mind. Yet, when it comes to confession, the confidence falters. I held myself with both hands, my innocence and truth being the only armour, in acceptance of whatever was meant to be forever hidden.

'Yes, King. I have a child with the sun god.'

I looked into his eyes, as Pandu probed into mine. When my eyes failed to convey, he asked directly. 'Are you in love with him, Kunti?' I shook my head vigorously, I'd never been in love with Surya.

'The mantra presented a mathematical complication. While solving the riddles, unaware of the consequences, out of my impatience to get done with it and be regarded as a genius, I made a computational error. It ended up invoking Surya, who explained to me the intricacies and bindings.'

A few moments of silence passed between us. Even the wild had taken to rest by then. Pandu asked, 'Where is the child now?'

'Under the care of his father.' I tried to remain calm, my heart thumping inside, a lump rising in my throat, praying quietly that Pandu wouldn't ask more. I didn't wish to expose my sandcastle to anyone. Yet, these were some questions I had to face, sooner or later. The heart racing and face determined to restore a ruthless tranquil, I felt Pandu's hand clumsily hovering over my palm.

Was he trying to empathize? I looked at him fiercely.

'Why don't you bring him over now?' He whispered, as the passing breeze gasped through the trees. 'Get him to join us, Kunti. No one will know. No one will be permitted to ask a question. You can count on me.'

Unknowingly, my other hand came forward to grip Pandu's. Where did this strength come from? I haven't known many, who would bend to this extent, even under the pretence of gratitude. Pandu wasn't trying to be grateful; he wanted to share his life with me, the way he could. By now, he knew that I didn't need him, even for survival. None of my desires could be met by any of his capacities. Perhaps, he even had an inkling that I desired something he couldn't possibly provide. But the pure intention to partner in a difficult chapter of my life touched me to the core.

I took a few moments for the tempting proposition to sink in, before shaking my head. 'He has already been adopted. He is growing up well. Pulling him apart will create a lot of noise. Meddling with a young boy's mind over something as existential as parentage would shake his faith. I can't. I shouldn't.'

Pandu frowned. 'You are a cruel woman,' I heard him saying. I couldn't agree more. I had been heartless once; but I couldn't be selfish now. Once you have let go of something, it won't ever come back to you in its entirety. Abandonment is unforgiving.

It happened when King Bharat was abandoned by his father, Dushyant. When both Vishwamitra and Menaka orphaned Shakuntala. When the twin sons, Luv and Kush grew up, away from Lord Rama. When the great Ganga left her child to her husband, King Shantanu. When Shantanu had let go of his son, Devavrath, transforming a youthful man to the self-renouncing Bhishma. It had happened in the past and it would happen again in the future, when my son would establish his life elsewhere, disowning his mother's pleas as a response to her Karma.

11

On that overcast morning, the sky looked dark, thunder cracking in the sky, releasing water in sheets. Madri, with the usual rhythm of her feet, danced around like a peacock in the wake of the rains. Her attire, half clinging to her body and the rest trailing behind, awakened the forest. Birds sang melodies, hiding below thick leaves, the ground smelled of fallen jasmines scattered on the wet soil, the heat moderated overnight, pains of the body satiated by the flowing water.

Pandu sat still, looking skywards. He turned towards her. She shone like the spark of a lamp, her songs assuring of ultimate unison after an interim separation. Leaving them both to their intimacies, I moved away to hear the first downpour of the season. For years they had been my celestial messenger, feeding me with the whereabouts of Indra but imparting no significant hope. Towards the end of summer, I would run down the plains from the height of my castle, every year, as soon as I spotted the black clouds afar. They would overpower the sky, swaying the trees and turning the plains white with the downpour. They would soak me inside out. But other than singing hymns of Indra, they would be unyielding to any additional information I might seek.

Once again, I stood in a secluded region of the forest, from where the sky was significantly visible. Thoughts of Indra never failed to transform me into the besotted teenager; from where I had started my sacred journey into romance. I closed my eyes, to feel the massive droplets drifting downwards over my body. Strangely, this time, I felt an attachment in them. They didn't just pass, they touched. In that trance, I clutched my elbow in anticipation. Was this Indra's invitation? Out of nowhere, delight plundered through my veins. Something in the air said the Devaraj wasn't too far away. With great contentment, I opened my eyes to the sublime nature, only to find Pandu standing at a distance, staring at me strangely.

'Why are you here?' I asked rudely, being forced out of the brief reverie.

Pandu came forward in slow steps, standing in front and looking intently at my face. Disturbed vehemently with this weird interruption, I pushed him away. He didn't leave.

'Who are you in love with, Kunti?' he asked, without removing his gaze.

This time my lips parted into a wry smile. 'What tells you that I am in love?' I challenged him, unwilling to give out whatever had kept me occupied.

'I know that expression well,' he said confidently, irrespective of my scornful remarks. 'There was a time when I longed to experience the pull of love, to be held with care, to seek pleasure in the beloved's arms, like everyone else did. I see the same longing on your face today.'

Taken aback slightly and embarrassed, I turned to walk away. With quick steps, Pandu stood before me, blocking the path. 'Tell me, Kunti. Who is this being, the thought of whom energized you to this extent? Who was your soul making love with behind the privacy of closed eyes? I must know.'

'Why do you want to know?' I asked, wishing that the man disappeared. I sought silence but Pandu was resolute in assuaging his curiosity.

'I have known you to be powerful, Kunti. I have seen you negotiating, agreeing, refuting, chasing – all to establish your dominance and might. You are never out of context. Neither hopelessly broken, nor overwhelmingly triumphant. For the first time, you seemed to have given up the reins. You were ready to fly with the winds. Who is the man?' he demanded.

What could I say about the love I had fostered for the lord of the devas? Would they ever know that the strongest is also the weakest, the triumphant is also a loser? That I have been rejected too many times but I was still alive to the hopes of a lover? Was there a language that could explain rejection to the man I had rejected?

'Not now, please.' I said and tried to run, but my wrist was held tight by iron fingers. Pandu pulled me towards himself, comforting me with his hands on my shoulders, allowing time for the breathlessness to settle. He knelt before me thereafter, making me spring backwards.

'Queen, by accepting there's someone to whom you have lost your heart, you won't seem rudderless. Love requires courage, it needs confidence.' Pandu said calmly. In his eyes, I saw no threat, no bitterness blaming the audacious royal wife for infidelity. It was only a complete confession he was seeking from me, just as he had submitted to me with his complete truth.

'King of the devas. Indra.' I uttered and snatched my hand free from him, to run as fast as I could, till I reached the spot where Madri was threading wildflowers into straw to wrap around her hair, humming a divine tune. Even the birds and bees were silent, listening to her in awe. Silently, I dropped myself beside her, my internal turbulence trying to settle into that music, undulating to the notes with beats of joy. My confession had made Indra's name reverberate in the air above. Burying my face between my knees, I wondered if the echo that touched every fauna in the forest, had at all reached the part of the world where the lord inhabited!

For the next few days, we spoke little. In fact, I didn't want to be disturbed and Pandu extended the favour of silence.

*

One hazy afternoon, I was alerted by the sound of footsteps moving towards us. All three of us listened carefully. Those were not the gallops of horses. Pandu picked up his bow silently and pointed in the direction of the footsteps.

'Don't,' I warned. 'They sound like three soldiers.'

'Not till I know who they are,' he whispered back.

Behind us, Madri had armed herself with needle-tipped stones within the folds of her cloth.

For my hands, she flung across a creeper with whetted leaves for hitting stronger than a whip.

All our preparations dissolved into Madri's shrill laughter, when the men passed through the woods to eventually emerge before us. We dropped our arms with smiles and tears. Bhishma had sent messengers from Hastinapur. Vidur had come with two other attendants.

Those were happy times for all of us to be united with the family. I asked about Bhishma and Gandhari and Dhritarashtra. Our thirsty souls were meted with news of well-being of father Kuntibhoja and Vasudev and Shalya. Gandhari had sent for us a great assortment of fruits. Pandu and Vidur took long walks in the mornings, talking to each other in the woods. Politics, economy, society and something more. I could hear the hum of their voices. I asked if everything was fine. Vidur assured me that it was, while Pandu looked away. I looked at both with sarcasm and got back to my chores. Pandu left in awkward steps and Vidur came forward to peel the fruits with me.

'Queen, the kingdom of Hastinapur needs an heir,' he said softly. I kept quiet, as I was expecting it to come up sooner or later. 'Bhishma is getting restless.'

I flared up in anger.

'Shouldn't this man find more work rather than peeping into other people's intimate lives?' I hissed, piling up a stack of dead leaves below a huge banyan tree. Vidur smiled at my exasperation.

'A kingmaker is rendered jobless when there is no one to be trained into a king!' he said calmly. 'What makes you so angry about Bhishma? Hasn't he given all his life to this land and its people, asking for nothing in return? No crown, no throne, not even a family! Shouldn't you be empathetic?'

I left everything and sat down, looking at him in the eye. 'When one gives up everything related to self, he either becomes god or a saint. Bhishma is neither. When you stay within the folds of luxury and yet renounce it with nonchalance, there is evil lurking inside somewhere. It raised its head when three sisters were abducted from their swayamvar, their beautiful garlands demolished under horses' feet, the happiness of that evening leading to a forced wedding with Vichitravirya, whose death made way for another sin of compelling the royal women to sleep with a sage, birthing one blind child and another impotent!' I gasped, having spoken too much in one breath. But I wasn't yet done. 'Bhishma's evil didn't stop there. It reflected in his upbringing of the two boys. Dhritarashtra grew up learning that being blind is as good as being dead by royal standards. And Pandu became a ruthless killer, taking great pride in the devastation he brought through wars.'

Vidur didn't utter a single word. He allowed me to calm down. We both heard the passing winds stealing the leaves and pollen, dropping them at their will, the bees struggling to keep their wings flapping under the exertion. 'Bhishma had raised three children.' He said after a while. 'But you map the great man's credentials on two, because those are the royals. Who is the prejudiced one, Kunti?'

I laughed and stabbed back, 'Me. And I will accept it before all, the day he gives the throne to the one more deserving – which is you!'

I didn't get much chance to speak to Vidur in the few more days he spent with us. But he spent a lot of time with Pandu. I knew what he was trying to convince him of. Not that either Pandu or I had not thought about it, but I knew this pressure coming from Bhishma was not the best thing to have happen. Pandu couldn't come out straight with Bhishma, neither would he accept that his children lived through his childhood. Before he bade us farewell, I packed for Gandhari my collection of medicinal herbs. Madri added to it her garlands of flowers which wouldn't decay too soon. To the richer sister from the poorer ones! Vidur accepted them humbly.

'As much as you are unhappy with Bhishma, Queen, you should know that his dedication towards the kingdom has remained the only marker of glory for Hastinapur in a long time. But perhaps, now the country deserves more reasons to smile.'

I kept quiet. He brought himself closer and whispered, 'Till the time Pandu is alive, no harm will ever touch your family. The stars are so aligned with Pandu's breath. Forgive the past, Queen. Save yourself for the future. It is going to be demanding and unforgiving.'

He left soon with broad steps. I kept wondering between my chores, why Vidur had said that. What did he want to indicate? And why the mystery of words? I kept looking at them from behind, till they were visible no longer. I still looked on, wondering whether our safety was good news for Dhritarashtra. Wouldn't he want all of us dead, so his disability didn't come in the way of the crown? I looked behind.

Pandu was crafting a seat of flowers and pretty leaves hanging from the lowermost branch of a tree for Madri. She had gathered black, brittle pebbles soaked in some flower nectar and set them on fire. Thin smoke filled the place with lovely aroma. Madri sat amidst them, bending a soft stem towards herself, squeezing its juice and painting her feet with dark scarlet, giggling aloud as Pandu may have made fun of her beauty regime. Even a rock would have melted at such a tender sight. Despite all their limitations and constraints, they looked beautiful together. While watching them with great affection, I took inaudible steps backwards, taking care not to disrupt their reverie.

Why couldn't I live in the present like them? Why was I born to be a perennial caregiver? Why did I hear obnoxious voices in the air? Why was I fed with every minute information, all that I was better off without knowing?

12

Lying below an ashoka tree, I could hear once again the voices from the future. Darkness brewed where light couldn't reach. As much as my sisterhood with Gandhari was pure, I could sense something notorious taking shape in our backyards. My premonitions were growing stronger by the hour. I had dreamt of a one-man army that evening, being attacked by a hundred vultures hounding him from all sides, pledged to tear his skin away from his flesh. The young man was all alone on the battlefield, with five shadows falling in five directions. The dust storm raised by his chariot was blinding. I covered my eyes, but not before identifying a peacock feather planted at its entrance, standing strong and undaunted by the fierce winds. Fearless horses smashed many; elephants trumpeted, declaring the end of time. Seated between the five shadows was Goddess Kali stationed on Vishnu's lotus, complexion as dark as the moonless night, clothes dishevelled, bloodshot eyes – laughing aloud before inflicting severe destruction. The chariot with the peacock feather circled around her with the intensity of a tornado. The warrior raided, ravaged and demolished whatever came in his way – while tears streamed down his eyes, burdened with irreconcilable pain in his heart.

That was my son fighting for Dharma. I was right there, behind him ... beside him ... before him ... but disabled from making any contact!

A cloud of air saturated with dirt and filth flew by. On the battlefield, they stood with their hands tied, mouths muted with a tight bandana, held captive. Bhishma, Vidur and the royal guru, Kripacharya. Which undefined enemy could do this to the biggest warriors of the land? Where was Pandu? There was one more person standing with them – sublime and handsome, skin glowing like daylight – equally helpless but not imprisoned. I had seen him somewhere before; it felt like I knew him very dearly. Before I could figure, a hand from behind went up in the air and a huge sword came down upon him. I screamed hoarse and frantically rushed forward to stop them, but couldn't reach in time. Blood splashed across my face! I fell down with the sudden pain I had experienced once before, when the umbilical cord was cut while birthing Karn. This time it was horrific, devastating, mournful.

I sat up from my sleep, breathing noisily. It was morning already, but the sun god was not to be seen. It felt inauspicious. I gasped and moved away from the other two. It was, perhaps, time for us to take the next step ahead, to prepare against the dangers of the future. When Pandu woke up and came searching for me, I asked directly, 'How do you want your child to be, Pandu?'

This time, Pandu didn't falter. 'Every human wants his own flaws to be corrected by his offspring, so whatever is lacking in him is covered by his child. I am no different. I want my child to be the human incarnation of Dharma, the god of righteousness, of truth and death!'

I smiled and nodded.

'For a long time, Kunti, I didn't have any sense of right or wrong. Things changed after you and Madri held me by a governing rope. I would like my son to be strong and stable, following the fairest path, unbending to treachery,' he explained.

'Only Dharma-putra?' I offered the minimum, pushing Pandu to talk more.

'And Vayu, the wind god! I would wish my child to be physically strong, capable of lifting the mountains and uprooting the banyans. I want him to possess the strength of ten thousand elephants, to be a master with the mace, powerful enough to scare off wagging brains trapped in rotten corners.'

I knew where this was coming from. In silence, I accepted his ambitious planning for our future. He had asked for mental and physical strength, but he hadn't asked for intellect and empathy yet. I waited for him to tell me more.

The voice that interrupted wasn't the one we were expecting to hear. 'Ashwin Kumaras. He will bring us twins that excel in Vedic science and ayurveda!'

We both turned, surprised. Madri sat there, isolated, privy to our conversation.

Moments of silence descended upon us. Pandu was bewildered and I wondered whether she actually slept on those nights or pretended to, when Pandu and I spoke about ourselves, exposing our fears and strengths to each other. Madri looked nonchalant and pleasant, having assumed her rights as an equal partner to our dreams.

*

Too much was bubbling inside my head. Yet, there was the tranquillity I hadn't ever experienced in my lifetime. According to Madri, my skin glowed and my hair had grown thicker. Hunger pangs were acute. I was up and active as I had always been, but this time, I somehow desired to slow down and lavish myself in idle reveries. Much time had passed since I had chanted the mantra, inviting the god to fill my womb!

Madri was now dedicated to nurturing me, retaining the best for my nourishment, washing my hair and feet with great kindness, running around to arrange things at the slightest hint, putting me on a sabbatical. Perhaps that's how priorities change when you are preparing to be a mother. Pandu told us about his greatest wars and that of others he had known, elaborating on the skills of warfare and bravery, hoping the foetus inside was listening and would be receptive towards all that the father could teach him even before he was born. The excitement of would-be parents is childlike. I started my days with meditation, following it with a chant of slokas that reinforced the values of peace, justice, fairness, ushering rich wisdom of psychology and philosophy – precisely the resilience of the Brahmana. With Pandu and Madri as audience, I explained the interplay of *purusha* and *prakriti* in the unique blend of the physical, the metaphysical and the spiritual in the creative ecosystem. Purusha functions as the unattached, as a mere witness. It is the prakriti that leads the purusha towards knowledge and consciousness, making him react and restore. The prakriti bestows its abundance upon nature, taking the form of feminine leadership with the optimum mix of firmness and tenderness. It is the prakriti, producing soma rasa, which attracts the purusha into its inherent illusion. It is the same prakriti, whose soma can reenergize the spent.

'King, I want our children to receive your exclusive attention, instead of being spoilt by the luxuries of the palace. I don't want the gossips of the concrete to cast their soot on our children. Let them grow up amid the vastness of prakriti, deriving strength from its soma, till they grow up enough to master their own reins.'

Pandu smiled at the picture I had just carved, with deep affection.

'All children of the clan must receive formal training from the royal guru, Kripacharya. However, it would be my honour to be at their back, Kunti. I will dedicate myself to their upbringing. But –' he stopped abruptly, unable to decipher whether he should pronounce his thoughts to me or defer them for some other hour, since I was at an advanced stage of child-bearing.

'What is it, King?' I pushed.

'When our children have grown up to be persons of fair knowledge and power, I will seek your permission to end my celibacy, whatever be its consequence! When my purpose in the world is on its wane, but I am not yet out of strength, I would like to make myself available to my beloved for one last time, offer ultimate gratitude for everything she has given me, irrespective of the times when I couldn't fulfil her needs.'

Jolted out of breath, I clutched his hand with uneven nails digging into his skin. 'Do you know what you are asking?' My voice quivered.

Pandu gently placed his palm over mine, softening my hold on his. 'How can I not, Kunti?'

'What will happen to Madri? And to me?' I had seldom panicked.

With tears in his eyes and a smile on his lips, Pandu threw at my face the cruellest truth.

'The day I die, Madri will be dead, too. She might still breathe, but that isn't living. And for you, Kunti, nothing much would change. When I am no more, mother my children like a father as well.'

Our joint dreams had suddenly started looking like a negotiation. For days, I couldn't heal from Pandu's merciless demand. But time pacifies all. I truly had no space in their little world. While Pandu had handed over all his rights to me to shape his present and future, he had reserved a small recess in his heart for Madri, protecting her entitlement with great might.

I let go of him, and perhaps myself, too.

13

Below the large peepul tree, its branches intertwined with the boughs of the neem tree in front. I sat in peace and closed my eyes to call upon the powers, praying for times of peace and bliss as I took myself through the complicated mantra again. I extended my devotion and gratitude to Guru Durvasa before I began. Pandu sat somewhere close by, watching my penance, his mind wandering haywire but eyesight steady. He refused to blink, lest he missed any aspect of this unforeseen childbearing. He looked on with the unflinching desperation of the father to stay in touch, howsoever meagre be his engagement.

With a clean mind, I started spreading the mesh of slokas once again, traversing from one level to the next, smoothly. Strange that even after such a long hiatus, a catastrophe that made me want to forget every alphabet of the chant, it was as alive in my memory as if I had been practising it since ages. The forest ground had been washed by Madri this morning; not a single dry leaf rustled in my path. Swiftly, I made the diagram with a stone on the moist soil. I didn't have to stop at various junctures, confused at the riddles or stuck in the complicated interlock of numbers. Mathematics flew like a stream, opening each layer with magnificent ease. It took me three days to reach the final stage and I prepared to call upon the god. Suddenly, Pandu interrupted, his voice trembling.

'Kunti, call Indra!'

I flung my eyes open, unwilling to look at any human, should that be too distracting. But Pandu repeated, this time with authority and conviction.

'None other, Kunti. Call Indra. Our child will be born out of love, not from a compulsion enforced upon the mother.'

He sounded distressed, as if trying to rewrite his own birth-history, attempting to prevent a disaster to save the world from another version of himself! I stayed still, looking in front, unwavering, till he calmed down. Pandu breathed fast, inscribing in my heart, his presence in permanence.

'In your ambitions, Kunti, you have taken the lead to bring before us, whatever we desired and whatever is befitting. This time is yours, Kunti. Call Indra. Our aspirations will be blessed by your fulfilment.'

Even in that state of detachment, when I had sufficiently distanced from mortals and their emotions, my eyes watered. I closed my eyes to chant further. When the mantra brought me to the final juncture, I remembered the smitten woman running through the plains in search of her lover, amid fierce downpours. I raised my hands to worship Indra. Even with my eyes closed, I felt the clouds coming together, thunder cracking through them, the breeze moisturized and droplets falling from above like petals of flowers. The holy staff of the divine facilitated a grand welcome. Instantly, I started feeling deported, from the earthen land of forests and rains, rivers and mountains, leaving behind Pandu and Madri and all other companions I may have had in various corners of the dominion.

*

When I opened my eyes, I was in a beautiful countryside. A host of thatch-roofed cottages thrown around randomly, little lamps on every window, intricate designs made by hand near the doors and on the outer walls. Flora in dark red and purple, yellow and blue, green and magenta interspersed between the creepers and trees surrounding them. Fireflies flocked onto the barks of the trees. The restless burble of the stream flowing afar, raised unheard music waiting for centuries. The chirrups of tiny, mischievous birds competed with each other. 'Is this Indraloka?' I wondered.

This wasn't a palace with the splendour of jewels on the walls, as I had expected it to be. It was simple, unmanicured, within the abundance of nature; light and air flowing liberally. The tree of Kalpavriksha stood in the middle, mesmerizing the place with its fragrance. Its roots untraceable, the plant spread far below where my eyesight could reach. There was no ground below my foot! Everything was suspended; yet nothing stopped. Mystic, but not majestic. There was no heat, neither fatigue – just an overwhelming warmth that usually welcomes dear ones after a long separation. The million questions I had carried from earth to accuse Indra of his absence, also seemed recessed. There was no anger towards offenders. I didn't know where I was headed. But I could reckon that there was only one way I could proceed. The right way! I moved as my feet prompted, touching nothing and yet touched by everything. With each step, the blooms changed their colours, casting their hues on the path. I walked through the reds and pinks and violets and oranges and whites. There was unexpected peace, perhaps because there was nothing to possess. I could hear faint jingles of foot ornaments in the air. It was the most jubilant gratification of being. I closed my eyes, a tear drop tickled down.

Where was this contentment before? How did I feel so graciously substantiated?

I opened my eyes to a city of sparkling stars. There were no riches embedded anywhere. Everything was just freshly washed in the rains, brimming with energy, glowing with health. Beautiful little animals stood below gigantic trees, licking the dew like tiny diamonds dropping from the leaves. Birds in blue, white and golden raised a mayhem of their own, hopping from branch to branch, piercing the flowers with their beaks to collect nectar. Beautiful figures roamed around in their own rhythm – talking, giggling, sharing in their own mirth. The *gandharva*s and the *apsara*s. Breathtaking!

Silvery clouds before me had suddenly started rushing into each other, teased by mild winds – bonding, separating and rebonding. They made obscure formations and dissipated again. But with each collision, something magical was shaping up. My hair flowing all over, clothes threatening to unbind, mind joyful and heart throbbing, I waited for Indra to assume himself.

Body as sharp as the thunderbolt, the transparence of water in his cobalt blue eyes, broad-chested and charming, the Devraj came forward astride the dense, colourful clouds. He brushed off their remnants clinging on to his elbow, waist and shoulders with his palm. Soft feathery vapours, like pampered pets, flew all around him, celebrating their release but unwilling to give up on the ever handsome. Time stood still. I was lost to this glory, riveted by the robust figure that smiled through his warmth and spoke with his eyes. My feet refused to move as I looked ahead without hesitation – not bothered about protecting my infatuation from amused onlookers. There weren't many, really. Most of the living world – from nature to animals, para humans to devas – were as smitten by Indra as I! The fact that Indra knew it all, made him even more bold and lustrous, adding to his appeal. His right hand stretched forward for a delinquent invitation. He held me by the hand and we matched footsteps.

I didn't know where I was being led. But I was in the care of my beloved, the enigmatic god I believed to be mine, though I had no valid justification for doing so. With an impossible appetite to see him, hear him and feel him, I stared on as if there was nothing else around. Here I was, finally placed where I rightfully belonged, waiting for the lord to unwrap the only gift I had retained for him. Me!

Indra smiled indulgently. 'Amravati is graced by your visit, Queen Kunti.' He whispered.

'Is this Amravati?' I asked, breaking out of my trance.

'Shouldn't it be?' he asked playfully. I ignored it and walked forward to touch his arm.

'Why did you take so long, Devraj? Haven't I waited all my life, just to welcome you as my lover?' I uttered with the soul on my lips.

'Shouldn't you ask that of yourself?' Indra's eyes stooped below to touch my lips and come back. 'You made Indra negotiate his space with Surya. But I was always around, Kunti. I was there for you, within the boundaries you had set for me.' His voice was melodious, hair smelling of lavender. Every passing moment, I was soaking in this lavish spread, call it love or longing.

'No wonder you are the god of illusions. You can respond to allegations with riddles.' I said with a smile. Indra laughed out loud, like a rush of monsoon droplets falling unpredictably on the face.

'No, woman,' he countered. 'I am the god of illusions, because I don't really exist the way others do. Not because I am allowed to compromise on truth. I am the impulse of humans – raw and unpretentious. A rugged, unfiltered confession to the self. I am your internal desire. I am what you want me to be. I could be a charmer, a fighter, a loser or a loafer. I am your senses. I govern the *indriyas*.'

Somewhat shaken by those words, I took a few steps back. 'Aren't you Devraj Indra?' I asked sceptically, wondering what he was hinting at.

Indra stretched his hand forward to pull me closer.

'Yes, I am. I have my own identity of having demolished demons and committed great acts of bravery, though as a king, I have none. Devraj is the combined energy of the devas. I am the representative force of Surya and his son, Dharma; of Vayu and of Ashwin!'

'What does that mean?' I asked, surprised.

'Our union will bring you three children, Kunti. Son of Dharma, Vayu and Indra himself. Madri's twins with Ashwin Kumar will also be borne by you, because I can infuse the serum of Madri and Ashwin but can't place the foetus inside her body.'

'Why would you do this, Lord?' I shook at the tremendous possibility Indra had just pronounced.

'Indra had been there with you, Queen, when you had been inside the women's chamber, investigating the origin of Pandu's polarized personality. I was there to release him from the cobweb of dark illusions he was lost within. Together, we helped him find Madri, and wake up to himself,' he assured me. 'Your desires align with a social good. Your love for me is not just born out of feminine passion but is also an ambitious succession for a state, as befits a queen. Not only do you fill in for Pandu's inadequacies, but also for the kingdom's defence and its progress. The cosmos, hence, has come together to fulfil your wishes. A blessing that is reserved only for a Sati – the seeker of truth – a dreamer, a performer, an uncompromising negotiator for that very truth!'

Indra's hand rested gently on my waist, heating up my skin with his mere touch. I placed my palm around his neck, hoping to be caressed. 'Why didn't I see you before? Why didn't I feel you around? Is the face I watch now with awe, an illusion?' I clutched his shoulders with the tip of my fingers. Gently, Indra drew me closer.

'It isn't, Kunti. You didn't feel me before because you wanted to possess, not experience Indra. I can't be possessed. Just like Ahalya didn't. Because the idea of Indra doesn't exist in reality.' He explained further, confusing me more. 'Each face has a thousand interpretations, all of which are true. When you come to Indra as a lover, you will see me at the pinnacle of my grace and strength. But there could also be someone who believes in the indulgence of materials. Amravati will not look the same for her.'

'Where is the Amravati I heard so much about? Where is Vishwakarma's magnificent creation of Indra's abode? I see no splendour!' My question fetched another divine laughter.

'You wouldn't, because that is not what you desired. In all these years, your perception of beauty has changed. Riches don't allure you any longer, richness does.'

'What does it mean?'

'The moment you entered Indralok, you passed through three chambers. In the first chamber, you left behind your anger, greed and conflicts. In the absence of those, the second chamber exposed you to the music and fragrance you carry naturally but remain unconscious of, under the influence of self-manipulations. You found yourself as a manifestation of the incredible illustration of life. The third chamber brought you to Amravati, where you experienced divine happiness. Don't you see this three-chambered Indralok as Vishwakarma's incredible architecture?'

'Who are you, Indra?' I asked, perplexed, unable to fit him within the known realms of my knowledge.

'I am who you want me to be, beautiful woman. I am the conscious. Allied with Vishnu at every stage, because when impulse fails, the inner intelligence takes over. Vishnu is the inner intelligence, the subconscious. Our child will likewise be aligned with the human incarnation of Vishnu, the *nara* to the *narayana*, seeking divine guidance from the Supreme Being, whenever trapped in complicated webs of indecision. You will bear Indra's son – a warrior. Your brother, Vasudev, will birth Krishna, Vishnu's avatar of compassion, tenderness and love, and a deft politician with unrivalled proficiency to interpret the rules of the universe. Together, they will be known as the keepers of Dharma on earth, just like Indra and Vishnu maintain the celestial balance in heaven.'

My attire fell off. Indra lowered himself to take me back into his arms. He split apart a cage where labels and titles could no longer hold us back from an undefined freedom. His lips parted to let out moans of delight, revealing tender vulnerability, all wrapped up within his regal strength. My hands gripped his, not for release, but for stability of the body from the virulent current of a river surging through my veins – displacing and rebuilding my understanding of Indra. One transient body was savoured by the eternal, magnificently absolving the disparity between a human and a deva.

EPILOGUE

'What is a Sati?'

I had asked Indra on the magical evening that immortalized one transient life with a blessing that would be remembered by generations to follow. Once back to earth, I was no longer chased by that overwhelming need to possess Indra. My world had calmed. Strangely, the status of my relationship with Indra no longer mattered. That he had been a breathtaking lover was for me to devour in the memory of spent flames. That time was peaceful and liberating. So much so that it didn't end with our parting. I could still close my eyes and lose myself in the divine touch, bringing those moments alive!

Such is the power of the indriyas.

'Sati is the woman with great knowledge and power. She can see through people and time. With immense intelligence, she dissects the past to foresee the elements of the future. Sati is the fearless one, not intimidated by the might of the resourceful. Provoked by nothing and suppressed under no ploy, she rewrites destiny for self and others. Sati is a change-maker!'

Indra's lips dug into my skin, disabling me to voice any further queries. But our communication didn't stop. Even in the course of intense lovemaking, my soul was as active as my body, raising questions and receiving answers from the one that held me within his arms, his face buried into my shoulders and fingers pleasuring my waist. Between the surge of his masculine length pushing against my body, I also heard what went unsaid.

My abode was permanently sealed within the Syamantaka *mani,* that was once possessed by Surya and was now in the custody of Indra. The lord of devas would come back to the Syamantaka, every time a corner of the gem threatened to dilute its luxurious blue, indicative of my distress and suffering. The mani that was as precious to him as his heart, secretly caged the power of the soma he received from our union. It would keep him informed about the movements of my pulse. From Indra, I would never ask favours. Not even for our son. But the Syamantaka would disclose all.

I would be remembered as the ambitious strength of the mortals, that would never fall short of her energies in pursuing resolute goals for personal and institutional growth, even in the face of enormous risks or self-defeating humiliation. History would celebrate me with pride, along with four other women who braved unpredictable demands of life without compromising on their dignity. One of them is Ahalya, another would be my daughter-in-law, Draupadi! Hymns would claim that reciting the names of the Panch Kanya – the five learned women – would dispel sins. Newer traditions would imprint us on a yet higher pedestal, the Sati, honouring our devotion and integrity to be among the purest ones to ever have inhabited this planet. Sati is the visionary seeking partnership with elements of the humane and the spiritual that curate spectacular benchmarks furthering the boundaries of physical and philosophical realities.

*

The greatest accomplishments are accompanied by the biggest pains. It was a night of tremendous discomfort.

I tried to contain myself, unwilling to lose control and share the agony with anyone. Nothing in my lifetime had ever made me forget that I was born to be the ultimate matriarch in history, dismissing Bhishma reinforcing the decisions for our future, all by myself. On this gloomy evening though, even the wild boars rested in silence, when I screamed in labour.

Pandu massaged my head, Madri brought warm water. Yudhishthir, our firstborn, woke up crying. Bhim, his little brother, turned sides and went back to sleep. Madri ran to take care of them, while Pandu attended to me. Towards the morning hours, another sharp pain jolted me from the inside out. I pushed hard.

I had a premonition that the third son of mine would be my dearest one. Pritha, the girl I was born as, would share her name with this one by some divine connection. He would be identified as Pritha's son, Partha. In spite of being the third-born, he would rule all royal decisions and also those of the battlefield. Like his father, he would derive resilience from the feminine to strengthen himself with emotional energy – a power that would silence the naysayers in the women's chamber forever, demolishing all those evils that had plagued his foster father, Pandu. Women would love him and rivals would be wary of him. He would be known for unparalleled bravery, simultaneously seeking wisdom and questioning it, too.

I held my breath and pushed again.

With my glory and Indra's, amid blessings showered from heaven, Arjun, the greatest warrior, was born.

ACKNOWLEDGEMENTS

It is difficult to acknowledge the people and moments that lead to a book of this order. I can name a few here, but what about those million experiences as a woman that made me go back to the past to question what brought us here? When history couldn't answer everything, I entered the terrains of mythology. And I discovered that a lot of women's struggles today result from the way the stories had been told while passing through various patriarchal epochs. The stories of feminine legends have been overlooked generously for patriarchal convenience, inspiring the woman to celebrate the bravery of only one section of the society and feel guilty about her own. Who and what do I acknowledge for helping me resolve that predicament?

The Sati series has received tremendous love from the Pan Macmillan India team. My heartfelt gratitude to Isha Banerji, Teesta Guha Sarkar, Bharti Taneja, Ditsha Gupta, Vijay Sharma and Rajdeep Mukherjee, for making it what it is. My thanks to Dr Prasun Chatterjee for initiating the work with *Ahalya* and to Misha Oberoi for the wonderful covers.

Dr Bibek Debroy has always been generous and prompt in extending his huge knowledge, every time I am stuck with confusion. No words can return such benevolence. I can't thank Dr Saikat Majumdar enough for his incredible inputs as one of the first readers of the manuscript. A lot stands corrected from their feedback. I also thank Sai Swaroopa Iyer, whom I go back to every time I need to verify my hypothesis.

I owe my gratitude to Hari Kiran Vadlamani and Indic Academy for putting together a brilliant network where everyone supports and learns from one another.

Many thanks to the senior authors, friends and readers who have loved reading *Ahalya* and have been vocal about their wait for *Kunti*.

My mother, Ratna Dasgupta, maternal uncle, Ashish Kumar Dasgupta, and father-in-law, Amarendra Kumar, keep me inspired by diligently reading my works and sharing their thoughts. Tuhin A. Sinha, my husband, has made many of the womanly battles non-existent in my life, with his own feminist perceptions and compassion.

Lastly, my son, Neev Tanish – I am an author because of him. I hope he grows up to be a fine human being and takes his mother's stories forward with his own contributions towards crafting a better world for women in the days to come.

ALSO IN THE SATI SERIES

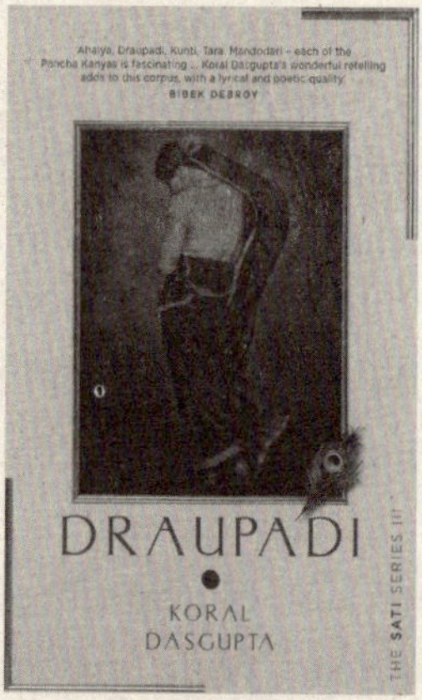